CARNIVAL
OF THE
DAMNED

Edited by
Henry Snider

CARNIVAL OF THE DAMNED

ISBN 13: 978-0692247815 (Evil Jester Press)

Editor: Henry Snider
Layout and Cover Art: Scribe Imagery / Henry Snider

Printed in the United States

First Printing, July 2014

1 2 3 4 5 6 7 8 9 10

Dedicated to the freaks of the world.

TABLE OF CONTENTS

THE MIRROR

TRACY L. CARBONE

"Think we can pull it off?" Danny asked out of the corner of his mouth, grunting as he carried half of a very heavy wood framed mirror. With a cigarette balanced between his lips, he squinted his eyes to avoid the smoke.

"Yeah. Shit, yeah. Set it down here." Gary's hands sweated and the wood slipped but it was fine. It landed right where he wanted it to, against the wall of the newest sideshow attraction at Bart's Carnival. His t-shirt was soaked and sweat circles spread under his arms and man boobs.

"You think this is gonna work?" Danny took a long last drag of his butt then flicked it onto the ground. Danny always looked cool and dry. His teeth were yellow and broken but so long as he kept his mouth shut, he was a good looking guy. Gary didn't swing that way, but the ladies certainly seemed to like him. He'd left a long trail of broken hearts over the years. "You paid a grand for this thing? Gonna take a hell of a lot of admissions to make it back."

Gary smiled. "Don't you worry. I give it a week."

"Whatever you say, Boss. At two bucks a pop it's going to take more than a week. Know how many customers that would take?" He counted on his fingers and Gary rolled his eyes.

"Five hundred. It would take five hundred customers."

"Yeah right. Five hundred. In a week?"

"This isn't just any old sideshow attraction. I'm playing for keeps. I haven't told you this yet, trying to keep it under my hat, but Daddy said if I prove myself then the carnival biz comes to me when he goes."

"Daddy Bart is dying?" Danny had been with the carnival so long he was part of the Carny family, even if he wasn't blood.

"No, no nothing like that. But he wants out. Wants to go to Florida with Step Mom Number Four. It's between Billy Junior and me. Whoever proves themselves gets the biz, gets to be the big boss. You know he always liked Billy Junior better but this time, I'm gonna win." The sun beat down on Gary's head and heated his whole body to an even higher temperature. Sweat poured down his legs and it looked as if he peed his pants.

"And you think this old mirror is going to do the trick? Beat Billy Junior out of the race?"

Gary leaned the full-length mirror firmly against the wall of the small cubicle decorated with faded red velvet curtains. This was the shabbiest spot in the whole set up but it didn't matter. Once they got people inside, well, it would be life changing. And those customers would spread the word. Next thing Billy Junior would be crying in his beer and Bart Carnival would be legendary. And it would belong to Gary.

He traced his fingers across the intricate carvings on the shiny dark wood of the frame. Gargoyles and creatures without names or definitions surrounded the hazy glass. The guy at the antique store said it was four hundred years old, from Romania. "Gypsy Mirror," he'd said.

"You ever have someone in your life you wished was dead?" Gary asked.

"Sure. Who doesn't?"

Just then the lights of the carnival turned on all at once. Strings of hanging bulbs in bright colors glowed and filled the summer night. Tinny circus music blared from loud speakers that had traveled with the carnies, with the rest of the gear, in hundreds of towns for sixty years. It was scratchy and warped but it represented home for Gary and so many of the others. Gary smiled and shut the curtain. Only a small clamp light with a red bulb illuminated their booth.

"You got someone you wish was dead right now?" Gary tugged on Danny's sleeve and stood him in front of the mirror. "Take a look."

Danny and he stood watching their reflections. A thick haze frosted the glass. That antique store owner had sworn on his dead wife's soul that the haze was made of souls, and that it was indeed a magic mirror, not a piece of junk. If not, Gary would have walked out of that store a thousand dollars richer and without a strained back.

But he *believed*. He'd seen people in the mirror, people not standing over on his side of reality.

Of course now it was just Danny and him, no extra folks, and he felt boondoggled. But maybe—

"Donna would be a good start. She stole all my CDs and two cartons of Marlboros and then she ran off with my kid inside her. Then she calls me from San Antonio and tells me it wasn't my kid after all. Wouldn't mind seeing her pass from this world."

This mirror magic was either real or bullshit, and Gary would soon find out which. He reached behind it and retrieved a tube about as long as a pen and thick as a highlighter. The end looked like a socket. "This is the key." He felt around the top of the mirror for the hole. "Got it." He had to play around with the key the first time but then he got it to fit and it snapped into place.

"What the hell was that? You break something?"

"It's spring loaded, I think, and has to lock in place for it to work."

"Okay so now what?"

"Look into the mirror, past all the streaks. Imagine Donna's in there."

"That's crazy talk, Gary. You off your rocker?"

The air got a chill to it and his sweat grew so cold it stung. "Look there, see the graves?" Before their eyes, just like in the store, row upon row of gravestones appeared in the mirror. Men, women, and children in varied states of decay gathered in front of the stones, a mass of undead looking back at them, hunger in their cloudy eyes. They all carried what looked like ski poles. Even the kids. The image was in grainy black and white and there was no sound, as if they were watching an old silent horror film.

"Holy shit, what is that? Who are they?" Danny turned around expecting to see them in the flesh, but there was no one extra. Just the two of them in the tiny red booth. "Who are they, Gary? What are you pulling here?" He tried to pull the mirror toward him but it no longer leaned. It had fused to the back wall. It throbbed and the wooden beings on the frame came to life, snarling and hissing, lashing out claws.

Danny backed off. "What the hell is this?"

Gary smiled. "Don't be afraid. You see this slot up here?" At the top of the thick wooden frame, a three-inch fleshy pulsating hole splayed open like a mouth.

Danny leaned closer to check it out. He rubbed his finger across it and yelped. "Damn thing bit me."

"Sorry. You got a picture of your ex still?"

Danny shrugged. "Why would I still carry about a picture of—"

"I know you better than that. You got a snapshot in your wallet or not?"

Danny dug out a well-worn and faded photo of Donna.

"Go ahead, put it in the slot and see what happens." Gary hoped it worked. Otherwise he was a big old sucker with an empty wallet.

Danny leaned over, past the growling goblins on the frame with their hissing tongues and yellow eyes. He dropped the photo into the slot.

The creatures quieted for a moment, then they purred and murmured.

Just then Donna appeared in the mirror, first as vapor and then in solid form. She was confused and frightened. When the others descended, her terror was clear. The corpses weren't slow and steady like zombies, more like a pack of hungry dogs overtaking a meat truck. They stabbed their poles into her, all taking frenzied turns to pierce her skin.

She screamed but no sound emanated from the mirror. The images disappeared and Gary and Danny were left looking at the cloudy reflections of themselves.

"Well that's just parlor tricks, Gary. Don't mean nothin'. It's a computer game. Am I right? Scans her picture and puts it in a video or something?"

"Wait and see, Danny, wait and see."

Gary knew it would work. He believed the Gypsy legend; but even if it was a fake, it sure as hell looked convincing. And that's what this business was all about. Entertainment. Giving people what they wanted, what they couldn't get anywhere else. Some came for the cotton candy or heart-attack sausage sandwiches. Some wandered in for the bright lights or shaky rides, the fun house, the sideshows freaks. What no other carnival offered up yet was the thrill of granting revenge. Even if it didn't work at two bucks a pop, hell, make it five bucks, someone would believe they'd rid themselves of an enemy. Even if it was an illusion, think of the joy they'd have till they found out.

But Gary believed. Sales might be slow at first, but the proof was in the pudding. If this was a legit revenge mirror, they'd make a fortune tomorrow night and Gary would be the future inheritor of the Bart Carnival.

Danny's big rough hands shook Gary awake. He sat up, startled, tried to get oriented. He'd fallen asleep in the tattered chair in their booth. Their second evening with the mirror would be starting soon and he hoped it went better than last night. They'd only had ten customers, including Danny.

"Jesus, you scared the hell out of me."

"She's dead. Donna's dead." Danny leaned against the wall. His hands shook as he lit a cigarette. "Her mother just called. Said they found her on the side of the road. Marks all over her, little bites or something, maybe rats. They don't know. Baby's dead too, obviously." Tears sprung to Danny' eyes. "What the hell happened to her?"

Gary's smile froze and turned to a frown. "You know damn well what happened. I thought this is what you wanted. You wanted her dead right?"

"Dude, not really. Not dead. I thought this was just a trick mirror. I was just playin' around."

Just then, Billy Junior tore open the curtain. "Showtime boys. You ready with your new attraction?" He laughed when he saw the mirror. "Best you can do? Thing looks like a piece of crap."

"It's not a piece of crap. Tell him Danny, tell him how great it is," Gary nudged.

Danny nodded. "Maybe we ought not to let people try it. I don't think it's safe."

"That so?" Billy Junior squinted his pig eyes. "Oh you guys are a riot. Not safe. That ought to attract customers. Enter at your own risk! Classic!"

He walked out and Gary followed. The nightly crowd filtered in and Gary knew he had his draw. "Hey everyone! Come on over and see the Carnival's biggest attraction yet! The Mirror of Vengeance! Destroy your enemies!"

A tired looking woman with a small son and daughter stopped in her tracks. She turned to him. Her left eye was swollen shut. "This thing real? Does it work?"

Her kids each held a hand and tried to pull her away.

"Mommy, I want to go on the Ferris wheel. You promised," the little girl said.

The woman ignored her. "Does it work?" She pulled both children into the booth.

Gary followed her. "What happened to your eye?"

"Does this work?"

Gary saw desperation in her eyes. Well, in the one eye. "Yeah it works."

"Stephanie, here's ten dollars. You take your brother to the Ferris wheel and don't leave there. I'll come get you in a few minutes. Don't you get out of the line or wander off, you hear?"

"Yes, Mama." The girl snatched the money then her little brother's hand and ran off.

"Vengeance huh? You wouldn't be swindling a single mom out of five dollars would you?" She sounded hard but her eyes and demeanor said otherwise.

"No Ma'am," Danny said. "It works but you best make sure you want someone dead. This ain't no joke."

She faced Gary and Danny. "Do I look like I'm joking? Bastard did this to me, he needs to die. If this mirror don't work either of you want to make some money taking him down for me?"

"What's your name?"

"Do I need to tell you that for it to work?" she asked with suspicion.

"No ma'am, just curious. Just a first name even. Or make one up. Just like to call you something."

"Name's Maggie."

"Gary." He shook her hand. It was small and moist. "Danny, why don't you stand watch outside? Maggie, do you have a photo of the person in question?"

Danny walked outside and shut the curtain. Gary knew this was good thing. Maggie would tell her friends. He picked up the rod and fed it into the hole. She jumped a little when it snapped into place.

"Put the photo right here in the slot and look into the mirror." Without hesitation she dropped the picture of a man in. "Now it's going to make some noise and the sides of the frame, well they're going to come to life but don't you worry. You just keep looking straight into that mirror."

A few days later, Gary saw a news report about the wife beater. He was found in an alley, hundreds of cuts in him, like rat bites the paper said. But Gary knew better. He zoomed in on the picture and saw the shape. << They were too even to be bites. Too perfect. The police knew this but maybe they didn't want to show their cards. Of course the police didn't say anything about rodents. That rumor was from the media, forging a connection between Maggie's husband and Danny's ex girlfriend.

Now all anyone talked about was the rabid killer rats murdering the citizens of Bradfield. Fine by him. He knew those poles the Mirror Folks carried were weapons. It made sense. He nodded, smiling.

Gary had actually run down to the local Staples and printed out some flyers.

<<LET THE MIRROR OF VENGEANCE EAT UP YOUR ENEMIES $10. <<

He'd put some of those little << on there to be subliminal. He read that's how all the big advertisers did it, like Coke, McDonald's and Marlboro. Little hints that went straight into your head and made you buy the product without even knowing it was a trick.

Word would spread, and soon enough he'd be a rich man and owner of the oldest family carnival this side of the Mississippi.

In a week's time, bodies were piling up. *My, what an evil town.* Bradfield was a quiet New England suburb, but boy did people jump on the bandwagon when they thought they wouldn't get caught. No one ever complained when Gary raised the price. He could ask a hundred bucks and get it.

From what one of Gary's customers told him, right before he paid his dues to eliminate his mother-in-law, the victim's bodies were drained of blood. This guy worked clean up down at the morgue and told the delightful details with wonder in his eyes.

"Hundreds of cuts in the skin of the victims. Hundreds stabbed in. Some deep all the way into the organs and some not much more than paper cuts."

It fit with that Gary saw the people in the mirror do. They all carried shiny silver rods and after a few minutes of chanting and hovering around their newest victim they attacked. The scene was always just out of focus for clarity but he was sure if he got inside that mirror, which by God he never planned to do, he'd see << on the end of their tools. The cops would never be able prove a thing, not a damn thing. The murderers lived in a mirror and the weapons were locked away with them behind the glass.

Their newest customer couldn't hand over his money quick enough. He even tossed in an extra ten bucks for "their trouble." After that, Gary left a tip jar next to the mirror and most everyone put a little extra in.

Gary grinned as Danny shut the curtain and stood as look out. Gary retrieved his key, put it in the machine and SNAP! The mirror came to life and soon they'd have another satisfied customer.

"You got something here all right, Gary." Billy Junior eyed the mirror. "You say you got this at an antique store?"

"That's right. Some shack on the side of the road in Maine. Pulled over to use the can and saw it. Next thing the owner tells me the history and I left with it in my truck."

"Always were a sucker. They saw you coming I suppose," Billy Junior said.

"Don't listen to him, Gary," Danny said. "He's just jealous because he didn't find it first."

Billy Junior laughed. "I ain't jealous. If I'm gonna spend a grand I'm gonna make it worth my while. The finish on this thing is shot. Can't even see myself." He squinted, rubbed his sleeve on the glass and stood back. "Nope, no value in this thing I'm afraid."

"He's just mad because Daddy Bart is going to give you the business and he knows it," Danny said.

Billy Junior shook his head. "Maybe so...maybe not." He spit a stream of brown tobacco spit into the corner of the booth.

"How about I put a picture of you in that mirror. Gary? Will that make you go away? That'd be about the easiest way to get what I want, I'd say."

A flash of fear struck Gary. *Would it? Probably.* "Of course not. It's *my* mirror."

"How about I turn you into the police?"

Gary laughed. "You want the police to come in here and sniff around? They'd shut down the whole carnival and then neither of us would win would we?"

"Suppose not." He spat again, this time right by Gary's foot.

"If you don't mind, I've got paying customers waiting out there," Gary said.

Billy Junior nodded and walked out without another word.

"I gotta take a whiz. Think you can man the attraction for a few minutes?" Danny shifted his weight from one foot to the other.

Gary didn't like that idea because it meant leaving the customer in there alone while he tended the crowd. But hell, it wouldn't take long. "Hey, nature calls. Go ahead, I got you covered." Danny walked into the throng and disappeared. A mass of people stood outside.

"Excuse me! Please, can I go first? Please!" A meth head elbowed her way to the front. Sores on her face, brown teeth, hollow eyes. But down deep she looked familiar. Who the hell was she? The other customers complained, one even shoved her. "Hey Buddy, no need to for that," Gary said. "She's just a little thing."

A red faced guy with a shiny bald head gave Gary the finger.

"Plenty of vengeance for everyone, don't worry. The Mirror won't run out," he said to Curly. To the addict he said "Sugar, why don't you just go back in line. It won't take so long."

She pointed down to her house arrest ankle bracelet, courtesy of the Massachusetts Correctional System. "Ain't got much time. Please, mister. Please."

He led her in, she paid, she dropped in the photo and he inserted the key. Her eyes filled with wondrous merriment. Not fear like everyone else. She smiled like a child. Beyond the damage of the life she'd led he could see innocence. Way down deep. He recalled an image of her by a stream with him and Danny....

"Becky?"

She looked up from the movie playing in the mirror, the ghouls gearing up for a feast, swaying by the gravestones. Yes, it was her. She'd been a damn sweet kid till the eighth grade. She'd gotten pregnant and no one stepped up as the father. She had the kid and gave it up for adoption. She never fessed up who did it to her but after that, well, she spent the last twenty years killing herself one hit at a time. Everyone in the town where they grew up suspected her father, and when he blew his brains out, it sure as shit looked like a confession. She never said different. Poor girl.

"How you been?" Gary asked. His heart broke for her.

"How the hell you think?"

They both turned to the mirror. The victim came into view.

Finally, poor Becky could get some closure. "Holy shit! That's Danny!" Gary shouted.

Becky nodded sadly. "Sure is. He never admitted it. What we did. Said the baby wasn't his but it was. I was a virgin when we did it." The folks in the mirror chased after Danny. He put up a good fight, but once the Mirror Folks attacked him, he went down pretty quick.

With trembling fingers, Gary reached for the mirror and pulled the key out. The murder vignette disappeared and in its place stood a satisfied Becky. Gary, at that point, looked like one of the dead.

"Get out!" He grabbed her thin track-marked arm and forced her out of the booth, the red curtain covering her like a shroud until she broke free and was just a meth head with a vendetta again.

"Danny!" he shouted as he knocked a fat woman out of the way.

"Watch yourself!" she yelled, but he was long gone. He stopped breathless at the row of Porta Potties. He had so many sweat stripes on his t-shirt it looked like a rugby shirt.

Gary rushed past the others standing in line. "Danny, you in there? Danny!" He knocked on all the doors.

"Hey, wait your turn!" The man who stopped him was so tall that all Gary saw of him was a giant forearm covered with a cobweb tattoo.

"My friend is in—"

A man screamed from behind the potties, by the tree line. It sounded like a dog being beaten. A yelp and high-pitched shriek of agony. Gary burst past the big arm and ran ahead.

Danny was cowering against a tree, thrashing his hands at assassins no one could see. Gary watched as bite marks appeared on his friend's body, stabbing through his clothes, deep into his skin. Not bite marks, no. Not rats. Tiny triangles just like the others.

"Make them go away!" Danny yelled. "Please make them stop!"

His hands continued to bat the empty air.

Why are they still there? I turned the key in the mirror. I took it out!

He patted his pocket. "Damn it!" No key in sight. Had he dropped it? Did Becky put the key back in?

Danny left Gary and ran to his booth. He tore open the curtain and saw the scene playing in the reflective glass. The Mirror Folks stabbed Danny's body, over and over. All of them with their poles....

Becky, Billy Junior and a crowd of others watched in awe. Sick fascinated smiles on their faces.

"This is some picture you got playing. What'cha got in there, one of them 3D video games?" Billy Junior's eyes were glued to the snuff film playing in the mirror. Gary lunged forward and ripped the fixture off the wall. The writhing demons slithered down the frame and bit his arm viciously with their sharp teeth. Their nails sliced through his flesh untill the bones of his hands were exposed. But Gary wasn't giving up.

With all his might, he smashed the mirror to the ground and shards of glass flew out and embedded themselves into everyone in range. Gary watched in horror as the movie continued to play in a large broken piece sticking out of Becky's neck. Blood oozed around it and the players were soon covered in a red film.

Gary pulled the piece from Becky's neck and stomped on it until the pieces were tiny.

People stood horrified. Some screamed, some called 9-1-1, and some took photos and videos. Gary ran off back to Danny. No one tried to stop him. They gave him wide berth.

Gary sat on the bed of in the camper he shared with Danny. It was a worn RV but it beat spending their profits on hotels. Danny had been Gary's bunkmate for as long as he could remember. They'd been through a lot together. Scads of women in countless towns across the country. More hangovers than a man could count, gotten arrested together a handful of times. Always butting heads with Billy Junior. A team, him and Danny. A team. And yet all those years he'd never admitted what he'd done to Becky. Gary shook his head, wiped tears from his eyes.

He looked across now at Danny, lying still in the worn bunk. Gary rose and walked over to his friend's bruised and broken corpse. Closed his eyelids. Ran his fingers over the hundreds of deep triangles carved into his skin.

No one was at the potties when Gary had returned. They were all back at the mirror, standing in blood, sending videos to Facebook and YouTube. As Gary dragged the nearly-dead Danny back to their room, sirens wailed in the distance. But he wouldn't let his friend die there. Danny needed to be in his own bed.

He sat now, watching Danny as the blood left his body in continual streams from all his wounds. There were too many cuts to stitch or cauterize. The paramedics couldn't save him. They could pump in all the blood they wanted, it would only come out. He was a human sieve.

No way in hell Gary was going to get the carnival business now. Daddy would let Billy Junior run it for sure. Gary would get blamed for all this death and rightly so. He'd bought the mirror. The whole carnival would be shut down. A sixty-year family business down the tubes.

A pounding fist against the metal door broke him from his thoughts. "Police! Open up!"

"Coming!" Gary stood up.

He opened the door and was shocked when the police charged and smashed past him. They knocked him to the ground. "You are under arrest for the murder...."

The officer continued the Miranda warning but Gary zoned out after the fourth name. How many were there? The paramedics looked up from Danny's body. "Better add this one to the list. He's covered in wounds just like all the others."

"I didn't kill anyone. It was the mirror," Gary defended.

A cop the size of a refrigerator hauled him to his feet. "The mirror huh?"

"Yeah. It was from a Gypsy or something. The people in the mirror, they did it! I just collected the money."

"And you just orchestrated it right? Coordinated the murders?"

"Well, I didn't stab anyone."

The cop yanked his cuffs, just to cause pain.

"It was just a silly carnival attraction, that's all." It never occurred to him he'd be an accessory to murder, but what if?

The cop laughed. "No you didn't murder anyone. Of course all the stab wounds in the victims match the weapon. And I'm sure your prints are all over it."

"What weapon? There's no weapon. It was all virtual."

"Save it for your lawyer. All I know is that the key your brother handed over to us, the one you used to turn the mirror on has inch-long razor sharp triangles on the end. Spring loaded and bam! Wounds, just like those on your buddy over there, and all the others in Bradfield who've been showing up dead. Funny thing, they even match the shapes in your flyers. Not too smart."

"But it wasn't me! I didn't even know the people who died!"

"But you had pictures right? You knew who to look for, knew what the victims looked like? Some people will go to great lengths to make money but that is just sick what you did."

That's not how it was. It's not how it happened.

Reality was closing in, tightening its hold on him just like the handcuffs that grew tighter each time he moved.

Maybe they'd shut down the carnival, but boy would business boom once they opened back up. *Son of Carnival Owner becomes Mass Murderer.*

No way to prove the mirror did a damn thing. Especially now that it was shattered. No way to show it to the cops so they could witness the ghouls in action.

"You got anything to say?" the cop asked.

"I'd like a lawyer," Gary said.

The cop led him in cuffs across the grounds of the carnival. People stared and took pictures. News cameras had arrived as well but knew not to get in the path of the police. As they passed by the attraction for the Mirror of Vengeance, Gary glanced over. Daddy was there standing next to Billy Junior. Daddy shook his head in shame, muttering something Gary couldn't hear.

"I win," Billy Junior mouthed.

A Sketch of Evil

Justin Short

Juan became a roustabout at sixteen, in the first years of the reign of Gregory Peck. It took him a few attempts to get the gig. He learned a fellow couldn't wear a tie and bring a crisp résumé to the carnival grounds…no, you had to get your face dirty and start fiddling around with heavy machinery until people assumed you worked there and paid you accordingly.

Roustabouts impressed him. Always had, ever since childhood. Seemed to be a different breed. His first glimpse of one was at a grade-school carnival. The man dangled from the rigging of a Ferris wheel, chewing tobacco with one side of his mouth as he kissed a brunette with the other, all while upside down.

They were always pulling stunts like that. Just yesterday, one of the nameless roughnecks was hammering around on the carousel when he discovered a wasp's nest. The man took a length of plywood and smashed it to the floor, then stood there like a blue idiot while the insects swarmed him – didn't move as they covered him

19

in stings. Finally he stepped away from the ride, face red and checkered.

"Whassa matter with you?"

The worker scratched his head. "Thought them'uns was mud daubers. Daubers 'ey don' sting or nothin' but I s'pose I was wrong 'bout 'em."

Straight from the mouth of the man responsible for making sure kids didn't die on all the dangerous equipment.

On breezeless days, Juan spent his time in discussion with other roustabouts. Usually nothing in particular – dames and cigarettes, Europe and the heat…stuff like that. Two of the older men typically curled their lips and reminisced about the war; threw their heads back as they tallied the number of Germans they'd killed, spoke in whispers about the German broads they'd romanced. Course, even Juan knew they were lying, but figured it wouldn't be polite to call them out on it. Let the geezers blow.

At least the boss was a decent fellow. Long-haired man, bald in the middle, cheeks like Santa. Bad thing was, Juan barely got to know the guy. Only worked for him two days before he up and disappeared. Just vanished one night. No words of goodbye. Nothing.

Juan noticed Bill motioning to him from the edge of the circle, so he got up and joined him. "Let's go," Bill said. "If I have to hear Virgil's story one more time, I think I might have to give 'im a good cussin'. "

Juan laughed. "Which one? The one where Churchill personally thanked him for his service?"

"Nah, the one where he snuck into Berlin and mooned

Himmler."

"Oh yeah."

Juan followed him around the Ferris wheel and onto the stomped-out path that led past the games of so-called skill. They stopped at the dart toss booth where Bill leaned in and made sure none of the balloons were too large. Good. Most of them were limp, barely inflated at all. Juan, meanwhile, ensured the darts were dull.

They stepped back into sunshine and made their way to the target-shooting booth and the duck pond. Rifle inspection. Bill's theory was to load two blanks for every genuine shot, then mock the customers and call out encouragements like "must not be aiming it right" or "we got a barn out back, want to take a crack at it?" Juan didn't argue with his method.

Finally they arrived at the baseball toss. Bill had previously shown him how to put just enough glue on the milk bottles so one or two might fall, but never the whole lot of 'em.

Juan gave a stack of bottles a healthy tug. Still fairly solid after last night. "So," he said, "what you think about the boss?"

"I don't know, kid. Seems strange he wouldn't even say nothin'. Few of us been workin' with him for years."

Juan nodded as he formed a new six-bottle tower out of some loose ones. "Kinda odd."

By late afternoon, the townies were flocking to the gates. The boss's absence didn't seem to matter; the place had to open.

Juan was working the duck pond. Arms crossed, he guarded the prizes and attempted to keep the children from shooting each other. Thrilling.

Unfortunately, a housewife he recognized from last night's carnival was still standing beside him. She'd been there half an hour and wouldn't leave. "I ain't no good at these games," she said while chewing her gum obnoxiously.

"All a lotta luck, ma'am," Juan said.

"Sure it is. My husband's at skee-ball. Thinks he's the expert."

"Hmm."

"Anyone ever tell you that you look like a Mexican Montgomery Clift?"

"Who?"

"Movie star."

"Ah. Don't got time for pictures round here."

"Well, he's sure a handsome fellah. Monty is, I mean."

"I better check on the rides, ma'am. Make sure–"

"Juan!" someone yelled. Juan turned toward the voice, grateful for the distraction. This immediately turned to worry when he saw the look on Virgil's face. "C'mon, son," he wheezed. "Emergency!"

He left the housewife standing, and hurried in the direction the other workers were headed. He dodged children and stepped on spilled snacks, nearly colliding with guests in the rush. Finally he made it, and saw the thing. It was kinda hidden in the shadow thrown by the Wall of Death, but there it was, all right. His boss, sprawled out in his suit and tie, a crusted red hole on his neck. A small Beretta, almost invisible in the dark, stuck in the mud beside him.

"Doggone," one of the men said, pulling his stained hat off his head.

Juan tried to catch his breath. Couldn't think of anything to say. Nothing to make the situation any better, at least. Doggone pretty much did it.

Two days later, a pair of strangers appeared on the grounds. One was a slender fellow with an out-of-place monocle. Dressed like a mortician. The second arrival was a gangly kid with thick hair and a creepy under-bite. They moved in unison, finally stopping near the hotdog stand, where most the roustabouts were assembled.

"Morning," the first man said, adjusting his undertaker's tie. "Got here soon as I could."

"You the replacement?" Virgil asked.

"Yes. The new foreman. Company put me on the first train out here. Terribly sorry to hear what happened, of course."

Everyone stared. Juan waited for Virgil to say something else, but he never did. Just stood there scratching his eyebrow. "Name's Johnny Kansas," the new foreman said, attempting to smile, instead giving them a disquieting, bared-teeth expression. "And my friend here is… well, I don't exactly know his name. He's mute. But he does great caricatures…quite the attraction for a carnival, you see."

"Eh."

Johnny Kansas tugged at his collar. "Well, the two of us should get settled in. Carry on, men."

When the strange duo was out of earshot, Virgil spat on the ground. "Tell ya one thing, that feller ain't look like no *Johnny*. And he's the funniest *Kansan* I ever seed. You catch that forehead? That's a *Ruskie* forehead."

An hour later, the foreman called them to a meeting. While the roustabouts sat in a circle out in the dust, the speechless artist squatted off to one side, scribbling furiously in a notebook. Johnny Kansas paced back and forth a couple times before facing them. "Men!" he screamed, raising his fist to the helter-skelter, "I have a new vision for our carnival. Something spectacular. We need to stand out, make a name for ourselves. So I say, let's build the world's largest tilt-a-whirl! It will be monumental!"

Juan raised his eyebrows.

Kansas shook his fists, mouth foaming. "No, not that…but hear me out. We'll construct the biggest house of mirrors in the nation – a manor of mirrors, hundreds of rooms and thousands of square feet. No! Wait! I have it! Picture a new Ferris wheel. Not your normal variety, but a quadruple wheel with cogs that interlock in just the right places."

Their boss threw his monocle to the dirt. "Stupid! That won't work! But how about a dunking tank, the largest known to man? Hundreds of thousands of gallons of water. Bigger than Lake Erie! Men, when we dunk someone, we want the world to feel it!"

He let out a stifled shout. Red-faced, he stomped away from them and threw open the door to the rarely-used kissing booth. It slammed behind him. Juan heard the click of the lock followed by Kansas's screams.

Bill had listened open-mouthed the whole time. Now it was over, he returned to his tobacco. Juan watched the man pass a gummy glob between his teeth. "Well," Bill said. "That was a sight, huh?"

"I'll say."

The artist seemed unaffected. Virgil took the opportunity and approached him. "Say, young man, I gather you do caricatures? Think you could draw me?"

The kid nodded, then ripped the current page out of his sketchbook and started slicing away at a new sheet. The rest of the roustabouts came closer. In less than a minute, the boy lowered his pen. He held out his drawing for everyone to see.

The picture wasn't Virgil, that much was for sure. Instead, a six-eyed thing stared at them from between the covers. Its body was massive and mammalian, with great wings protruding from its shoulders. It was mostly furry, but an occasional patch of fish scales decorated its hide. Seven sets of antlers adorned the creature's crown. The face was the worst, with all those eyes, and the pair of snarling mouths directly below them. There had to be fifty or sixty teeth in all. Juan found himself shuddering. It was so awful. Almost sickening. Unnaturally ugly.

Didn't seem to bother Virgil. He simply scratched his chin and shrugged. "I dunno. Don't really think it favors me."

Johnny Kansas never emerged from the kissing booth, so they set up for the carnival like usual.

Regrettably, it was Juan's turn to be on vomit patrol. He spent his evening combing the grounds, cleaning up after the weak-stomached patrons. Honestly, what did these people eat? He failed to see how someone could lose his lunch on the kid-friendly rides (*who threw up on a kiddie slide, man?*), but it happened.

Mrs. Housewife was here again tonight, but she kept her distance. Either her husband had given her a warning about mingling with carnies, or maybe that bucket of waste he carried was just that unappealing.

Or perhaps the artist was giving her the chills. He seemed to have that effect on guests. Earlier, when a man wanted a simple picture of his twin girls, he was rewarded with a drawing of dual skeletons complete with melted flesh and bulging eyeballs. And a few minutes ago, some kid paid to have his sweetheart's portrait done, and ended up getting a page full of winged nightmares. Not exactly good customer relations.

The kid had stationed himself in front of a cheap-looking tent, directly between the basketball toss and the bell-and-hammer game. Juan wasn't sure how many dollars he'd taken in, but he was *constantly* writing in that notebook. Never stopped to eat or walk around, just kept sketching, customers or not.

While Juan was scrubbing a multicolored slab of concrete in front of the picnic area, he felt a tug on one of his belt loops. He knew who it was, and wished she'd kept up with her silent treatment. No help for that now.

The housewife was all teeth. "Hi again."

"Uh, hi."

"Husband didn't come out tonight. Had to work."

"Can I help you find something?"

Her face flushed. "Don't act like that! C'mon, let's get our pictures did."

"I have to–"

"I'll take over," Virgil's voice said. The old man reached out and removed the bucket from Juan's hands. "Go on, kid, have a go at the artist."

"Where did you come from?"

Virgil waved him away, his face almost angry. "Have fun, now."

Juan led the woman to the mute's improvised studio. They took their seats on a couple folding chairs. His was smeared with cotton candy.

The boy flipped to a blank sheet and looked at them in turn, his mouth half-open. For the first time, Juan noticed how pale the kid was. He was distracted by the way the boy's bangs blocked half his face. Surely he earned enough to get a haircut. Before Juan got too lost in thought, the artist's pen was back in motion, his hand moving in wild zigzags and spirals on the page. His face was pure concentration. Drool spilled out his mouth, but the boy didn't seem to care.

Juan's lady friend could hardly keep still in her seat. She giggled and drummed her fingers on the metal backrest. Pretty annoying.

Not more than a couple minutes later, the boy grinned and handed Juan their portrait. He had expected something shocking and inappropriate, so he wasn't too surprised when he saw the finished product. On one side of the page was some sort of giant cobra with bloodshot eyeballs that was flashing out its tongue and dripping venom everywhere. Beside the snake stood a half-decayed woman, her face nearly gone, organs showing through thin skin. Her hair extended to the ground, where it connected to the soil like some strange willow tree or something. Behind the pair of figures were dozens of rows of tombstones.

His companion's face sank. Good, maybe she'd go home in peace now. "Awful, right?" Juan said. "You should see the one he drew of the mayor's wife."

She held her hand to her mouth like she was trying to stifle the urge to expel her last meal. He knew that look… goodness knows he'd seen it enough tonight. "Don't get sick," he said. "Please."

She shook her head and ran from the carnival without another word.

It was dark, and Johnny Kansas hadn't been seen all night. But finally, when folks were starting to go home, the doors of the kissing booth flew open and the boss leapt out. "I have it, men! I know our destiny! It's so simple…we add a rope climb challenge! It'll be tall as New York City. Whoever makes it up and rings the bell, we give him a prize. This'll bring 'em in. It'll be perfect!"

Juan wasn't completely sure he agreed.

The parts weren't supposed to arrive for two weeks. That left plenty of time to speculate on what was wrong with the boss…the odd behaviors. The way he flew into those fits of rage. Never actually struck anyone, just swung his fists around like an angry cartoon character before retreating to the kissing booth or tarot tent and sealing himself inside for several hours. The way he spouted that nonsense about building a monument.

Bill suggested he might be one of them hidden commies folks always talked about. "Do you know," he whispered, "I ain't never heard him say the Pledge of Allegiance?"

"Um," Juan said, "I don't think you've heard any of us—"

"Nah," Virgil said, dismissing the idea with a demonstration of long-distance tobacco spitting. "Ya always hear about those guys escapin' from chain gangs. Maybe ol' Johnny with his ludicrous idears is one of 'em. On the run from the law and what-have-ya."

It wasn't until they started construction on the support bars that any of them considered the horrible truth that he just might be an alien. That unnatural baldness, that hard-to-place accent, not to mention this monolith he was building. Its height was outlandish. Thousands of flashing lights ran up and down the sides. Around here, the gaudy thing stood out like the Eiffel Tower.

"This'll be a heap of fun to disassemble," one of the men said.

Juan groaned at the prospect. That wasn't a job to look forward to. And what about hauling the monstrosity to the next town? It would take a dozen flatcars, easy. Yeah, carrying this thing with them would prove to be quite the chore. Juan mentioned his concern to one of the workers, but the man seemed more concerned with the latest rumor about Kansas.

"Likely to be a signal for one o' them spaceships," he said, stepping past Juan to finish his work. The man did a final once-over on the concrete base while the remaining men rested on the bare dirt and gazed at their handiwork. Staring at the tower felt like looking into the heart of Vegas. It was beautifully frightening.

The night after it was built, Juan couldn't sleep, so he got up and walked out of his tent. Noticing an unusual smell, he took a couple steps toward the baseball toss booth. Lying on the countertop was a body.

Virgil! The man's stomach was bubbling and pink, his body nearly severed at the bellybutton. For a second Juan thought he was still alive, but then realized he was only hearing the dripping and splashing of his blood. He'd definitely been sliced by something, but no weapon was in sight.

Juan screamed. The men were at his shoulders in less than forty seconds. One thing about going to bed on a moving train…makes a guy a light sleeper. They crowded around Virgil's corpse, shoving and cursing.

Johnny Kansas and the caricaturist were there too. Seeming to feel the collective blame, their foreman threw his hands up. "I was playing cards when I heard the scream…it's so awful…poor fellow…"

"What about him?" someone asked, indicating the boy artist, who still had that infernal sketchbook in the crook of his arm.

"He was with me. No one else wanted to play."

The following evening, a third accident made most the men agree the carnival was cursed. As the Ferris wheel was turning along happily, a shriek lit up the night. Juan broke his concentration from the carousel. A woman was falling, arms flapping, skirt billowing. From her height, it was clear she'd slipped from the topmost car on the wheel.

Bill was on duty. Juan saw him rush for the middle, but there was too much ground to cover. She was a middle-aged stain in the dirt before he ever got there.

Juan arrived, out of breath, and recognized her immediately. It was his housewife friend. Guess she couldn't keep away from this place.

She looked pretty terrible now. Her dead eyes stared past him, and her tongue seemed to be trapped between her teeth. Blood trickled out the sides of her mouth. Juan cringed when he saw her arms and legs...they were all busted, shooting out every which way like some kind of crazy scarecrow. It wasn't quite decent, so Juan retrieved his blanket from the nearby tent and covered her. He felt like he should have been able to tell her name to the hospital folks and the coroner, but he just couldn't recall it. Real shame.

Of course the wheel was shut down. But that night a light burned up top. Seemed like the topmost car was glowing. It was queer, out here at midnight like this, but Juan had a feeling if he told anyone it'd disappear. He also knew he couldn't just crank the machine up and bring the car around.

Only option was to climb that skinny ladder on the side. He started quietly, trying to use his arms alone, barely letting the tips of his shoes touch the rungs. He never gave much mind to heights, but when a guy is sandwiched between tons of machinery, hoping the wind doesn't knock him off the suddenly-creaking wheel… well, it makes a person question his life's choices.

Thirty feet up without a sound.

Then fifty.

Finally, he was almost level with the car. He saw Kansas's shadow thrown against the backrest.

"…am serious!" he was saying, trying hard to whisper. "This is too much! Why do you think I left there? You think I don't miss it? But you've got to stop! Not here… not again."

A low answer came from the other side of the car. Juan couldn't see the speaker; he could only hear the voice. It was more like a moan. A scratchy, deep-bellied bark that sent a shiver through his skull. He couldn't understand a word spoken.

"I…I won't," Johnny Kansas said. His voice didn't sound as confident as it had a couple seconds ago. "You can't make me. No, not even you."

Juan started sliding back down the ladder. This wouldn't be the place to get discovered…it'd be a little hard to explain. He reached the base and stopped. No steps behind him, that was good. Just those same whispered voices followed by a muffled cry. He hit the dirt and flew to freedom. Sliding back into his tent, he proceeded to spend the entire night awake.

Finally the rope climb had its grand opening. It'd been completed for a few days, sure, but Kansas wanted to build the anticipation. People drove in from two and three counties away – flat as the land was, no doubt some of them could see the illuminated thing from their porches. Those flashing bulbs covered it, hundreds and hundreds of them, like a double Christmas tree leading to the heavens. A single length of rope extended almost out of sight, boring compared to the brilliance of the supports.

The carnival never had a better night. Thousands of tickets sold, almost as many hot dogs consumed. Lights flashing, children smiling, movement all around. And yet, the roustabouts stood dumbly around the base of the new attraction. Their boss was absent. So was the artist kid. No big loss there. Little weirdo.

Suddenly, a child pointed. Someone stood, arms outstretched, on top of the rope bar. A hundred feet above them. "Boss!" one of the roustabouts shouted, recognizing the figure as Johnny Kansas. He repeated his cry, as if one voice could be heard among the scrambling and screaming.

Not knowing fully why, but feeling like he was doing something important, Juan leapt onto the rope and started climbing. It brought back awful, sweaty memories of building this blasted thing. He trembled as he recalled the hundred-and-two-degree weather, the way he'd been suspended dozens of feet in the air, and how he fought to keep his grip on the welding torch even though it scalded the skin. Of course, the memory of last night and his brief stint as a Ferris wheel spy also came back.

Dozens of pulls later, he was just halfway up.

He continued, hands clawing furiously, not stopping to look down. Not cause he'd freeze up, just because it would waste time. Between gulps of air and rope-burns, the brightness of the bulbs nearly dazed him. The sounds of the far-off rides dulled. He thought, whose idea was it to build this ridiculous gym-class affair, anyhow?

Finally he panted and heaved himself atop the bar, accidentally dinging the bell in the process. "What are…

you doing?" he wheezed.

Johnny Kansas threw a hand back dismissively. "Go away, Juan. You're just a kid."

For the first time, Juan realized Kansas wasn't alone up here. There was the dumb kid, standing in shadow at the other end of the thin support, his arms raised in anger. Not surprisingly, one hand still clutched that notebook.

"It's him, ain't it? The kid? He's the one who's been..."

As if in answer, the artist tiptoed closer, not holding his arms out to balance or anything. His eyes were full and bulging tonight, pupils barely visible. "Who are you?" Juan asked, not really expecting an answer.

The kid stopped and sketched something for a few seconds. Juan was on the verge of telling him to forget it. He didn't need to see another being from someone's nightmares, this wasn't the time.

When he saw what the kid had drawn, thrown into light by the colored bulbs, his spit caught in his throat. This was far more hideous.

The drawing wasn't of some multi-armed being from beyond. Instead, it was a simple sketch of a man. A man with short black hair and a small, cropped mustache, an eerie frown, one arm raised in a familiar salute.

"That's impossible!" Juan spat. "He's dead! Don't you think I watch the newsreels?"

The look on Johnny Kansas's face made him stop. "It's possible, kid. The man himself died, sure. But that amount of evil, it's a little harder to get rid of. So that's where I come in. I can't let him keep doing this...don't care what happens to me."

"You'll lose," the kid wheezed in thick-accented English, his voice a creak, like it gave him pain to talk. "Dey always lose."

"Little brat," Kansas muttered. Then the monocled

man cupped his hands to his mouth and shouted something. Amid the cheers and cries from below, it was hard to distinguish. At first Juan though it was "Porcelain!" But that was stupid; that made zero sense. Of course he screamed "Deutschland!"

Not much of a final farewell, either way.

The two figures fought for a short moment above the rope, toes dancing on the slender metal, then both were floating away from the glowing monolith. They seemed to hover for a second. Then they careened, speeding toward an open-mouthed crowd, growing faster every second. The ground rocked like a firecracker had exploded.

When Juan made it back down, the body of his boss was on its back, almost unrecognizable in its bloody-spaghetti form. The kid was nowhere to be seen. No corpse, no fragments, not even a finger or toe. Just that notebook, thrown open to the last image of a man and his heil.

Juan quickly crumpled the terrible page into a ball and shoved it in his pocket. His eyes darted around; silently, he wondered where the Führer would surface next. Not like he had any way of knowing. For now, he patted the piece of paper. That'd make some good toilet paper later on.

Seemed poetic.

When the police sent the ticket holders home and shut down the lights, the roustabouts were alone. "I'll be," one said, "the boss done it. He weren't a alien after all."

"No?"

"Nah. It weren't a beacon. All this time we was buildin' his tomb. A monument, like he said."

Juan started to cry. "Should we…do we say some words?"

"Yeh. Let's do that."

After a couple minutes of silence, one of the men found the foreman's bloody name tag and tacked it up to the steel base. Nods all around. This was appropriate. After all, no one could think of anything meaningful to say. No desire to break the stillness.

And then, as roustabouts do, the men slipped away from the busted rides and condemned games of skill, moving through the night.

Another town, another carnival.

LOATHSOME CREATURES

AMITY GREEN

"Get out, get!" Elise yelled. It was a damned infestation. Frogs, or maybe they were toads, had moved in like the freaking wrath of God settled over Vancouver. She didn't really care which breed of slime crept and hopped into her gardens. Amphibians were retch-worthy.

Two nights ago the burping sounds started. Twilight was hours off on the third evening but the noise was enough to give her a mild headache and a twitchy eye. The second huge toad, or whatever, popped his sticky ass onto her porch and Elise let Tigre through the door. The cat scampered forward and mauled the frog.

I never thought I'd hear one of these disgusting things scream. Elise gulped, looking away. There was an enormous amount of entrails packed into the gut pouch for such a small creature. Little bones cracked as the cat dined.

No more frogs dared climb the two steps onto the tiled outer living area. The sound though, the bloody din of frog calls, low, airy barks and shrills alike, ruined the peace. At 1.5 million a half-acre track, the value of the land prevailed over frogs. Her not-so-modest home stood for more than merely a place to live. Elise was a career and lifelong bachelorette. Her little slice of the earth was a trophy for overcoming, remaining cast-iron, and working hard through her thirties. An impeccable yard, free of vermin, was her just reward.

Exterminators were finicky creatures and the two she'd looked up on her smartphone refused to come eradicate the gooey junk threatening her quiet. The last man laughed, telling her, "Frogs? You want me to come out on a Sunday, for two frogs, lady?" He'd beat her to the punch ending the call.

Two turned to four turned to eight, slime multiplying, growing, morphing, whatever, and eight short hours later Elise was surrounded by enough frogs to convince the French to emigrate to the States for brunch.

She curled her lip and left the cat to finish, fluffing cushions on her elegant chaise lounges as she retreated, then sealing herself behind the door. The thick wood quieted the yawp, but only a little. The outer foyer dimmed considerably by the moment. She clicked through the arch that marked the line to the grand entrance and popped on the oversized pendant light high above. Bliss was walking farther into the house to leave the sounds of *Wild Kingdom* behind.

A calming snifter of luke-warm brandy in one hand, Elise melted into a plush recliner that was big enough for three petite women her size. She sipped, eyes closed, and concentrated on peace and calm, sans frog.

Har-uh-uh uh uh. The sound rattled through the den and Elise shot from her chair like her ass was on fire. Brandy soaked her silk blouse and dripped from her chin. She stepped back into the chair, crouching low and slid free of her Italian heels so the leather wouldn't suffer a punch-through from her No BS stilettos. One of the retched things must have slipped past earlier. It wasn't fear that curdled her gut. It was disgust. If she put a bare foot down on one of the detested things, she'd be sick for a week. She wiggle-swung the chair in a circle, looking for the frog. From the volume of the thing's croak, it was likely a huge blop of a thing.

Elise stopped shifting in the chair and held until the movement stopped. In the soft light coming in from the kitchen, the fat slug of a beast sat on its haunches, staring, with its chin nestled into a fat pocket of air on its chest.

"Oh," she growled. Of all the ballsy moves. The frog watched her, uneventfully panting, the balloon underneath its chin growing and puffing out.

Har-uh-uh, it teased.

Elise looked toward the foyer. On queue, Tigre merrowed at the door, certainly hearing a new opportunity for dessert. She'd spare the cat, though. The last frog was big. The perpetrator in the kitchen archway dwarfed it. The cat would be sick from too much muck in his system. She wouldn't risk the possibility of scrubbing regurgitated frog out of the carpets. As much as she might delight in watching Tigre chew the frog, the task was on her.

The frog belched and watched as Elise peeled down from her perch, padded to the fireplace, and retrieved her weapon of choice. Iron poker firmly in her right hand, she stalked up and viciously bludgeoned the frog gleefully, losing her breath. She dropped the poker and grit her teeth against the clamor when it hit the tile. Embarrassed at letting herself go in such a fashion, she nimbled a loosened strand of hair back into line with the rest of her smartly cut bob. Without delay, Elise cleared her throat and stepped over the mess en route to the dustpan and Lysol, unwilling to let the goo gel while she waited for the cleaning service to get to it.

A loud rapping sounded through the house, jarring Elise. The aerosol can popped against the tile, sending the lid skittering under the breakfast bar.

"Dammit," she said, rubbing her sternum. Heart still pounding, she stomped back into her shoes, rounded the kitchen doorway and headed to the front door. She cracked the door a wedge, ready to stomp anything that attempted to hop inside. There were no frogs in sight so she flung open the door, glaring.

"See this?" She gestured toward the doorbell. "It's a door chime. People in the civilized world use them to call upon a home without pounding on a twenty-three thousand dollar, heirloom front entry."

"Apologies, ma'am," the thin man said. He peered down with wide, blackish-brown eyes. A green ball cap contained most of an outcrop of salt-and-pepper curls. A matching Fu Manchu darted from his pointed chin, pointing down toward a V-neck tee beneath a brown jump-suit. On hand clutched the handle of a five-gallon bucket with a dingy canvas organizer hanging over the edge. "I'm Vic. Carousel Pest Control." He jabbed a thumb over a shoulder and turned to open the view to a van marked with a gaudy depiction of a dozen mad clowns on a roundabout toy, wielding tanks and spray nozzles. A few oversized dead roaches lay on their backs, legs up.

"Stan over at Acme called you in. We work their off-hours gigs. What variety of pest do you need help with?"

"There, do you see?" Elise pointed to the drive way where a cluster of little frogs infiltrated an ivy bed. "And in here," she said, stepping back so the man could enter. Once he was past she closed the door firmly and led him to the dining room arch to show him the flattened frog. "There must be a million of them. All sizes, and increasing in brazenness."

The exterminator bent over the dead frog, setting the bucket down with a thud. "Did you smash this guy?"

"Guy?" Hands on hips, she shook her head, wide eyed. "What the hell?"

"Didn't mean a thing by it. Rest assured, I'm here to help with the pest problem." He reached for his bucket.

"That would be the point, now wouldn't it?" *Idiot.* What could she expect from a forties-ish man who held such a job?

Vic pulled a black hand gun free and stood. "From one prospective, certainly." He leveled the weapon at her and squeezed loose a small dart that firmly lodged in her shoulder. A second punctured her neck. Elise shuffled back in a frenzy, her backside colliding with a chair. She tripped and smacked the tile, woozy, unbelieving, and weak.

"What...what," she stammered. "The frogs, moron! Not me!" She turned to run as he answered with another dart that lodged into the meat of one cheek.

"What...the hell?" he ad libbed.

The view of him narrowed to a tunnel. Elise blinked, trying to hang on. It was no use. She curled into the tightest ball she could and let her eyes close as her head hit the tile.

The smell of dirt and salty, dried animal dung awakened her. Happy music, reminiscent of throwing darts at a bright wall of balloons, played from a PA system in the distance. Applause and gleeful children squealing increased the pounding in her head. Dirt fell from her lashes when she sat up. She let herself rest against a row of metal bars beside her. A line of vertical rungs surrounded her, leading to a door with a black metal latch.

A man in a pastel striped clown suit clunked by in the cage next to hers, oversized red shoes kicking up dust and legs pumping as if he was running through a waist-deep flood. Stopping just before the front bars, he shook loose of enormous, white gloves and let them fly. His hands were thin and pail, barely masculine, and nearly as anemic as his painted, glowing face. He crossed his arms and shoved his hands into his armpits. The gloves landed with a dusty plop and he whipped an about-face followed by a floppy-shoed dash to the back boards. Bloodshot eyes searched for anyone watching and when his breath slowed, he removed his hands, beholding two fresh, fluffy gloves.

"Mmph," he whined, shaking his hands to peel off the new gloves but they stayed in place, as if sewn to the sleeves of the colorful onesie. The whimpers became full on squeals and he dropped to his knees, yanking puffs of green, blue, and purple hair free from a bleeding scalp. Fresh crops of multihued, tightly curled hair replaced what he ripped out within seconds. Barks of insane laughter punctuated each fresh scream. One hand squeezed hard on his bulbous, red nose, sending bleating horn beeps into the fray.

"Help me!" he yelled. "Ha ha haaaaaa!"

Insanity settled over Elise in the form of hysterics. A sob built but she swallowed it down. She would not allow herself to act out like the man next to her. Dignity would remain. She would simply free herself and go home. Better yet, she'd wake up from the nightmare, make some tea, and be off to work.

The clown grasped the bars between them with bloodied gloves and beat his forehead numerous times against the iron. Bloodied teeth shone streaked pink inside a painted red grin.

Elise crab-stepped away in a frenzy. Being a strong woman was one thing. Fighting complete loss of control from terror was a whole different breed of cat. The sob broke free, traveling up her throat and getting caught there. The pressure grew intense and each time it felt as if she burst out into tears the soft flesh beneath her chin stopped it. She whipped her head from side to side, attempting to release the sob that by then had grown into a scream by the feel of it. Swallowing didn't force it back down. Numbness in her feet and hands and numerous hot flashes didn't help her confusion. Refusing to give in to hysteria, Elise breathed in through her nose and out her mouth, getting to her feet and smoothing her outfit into place.

"Excuse me," she called down the walkway. "I think there has been a mistake made here. I've been locked up in a cage and someone had damned well better be over here to let me out, pronto, people."

No one answered.

"Okay, look. I know there has to be someone who can hear me. Just c'mon over here and let me out and I will not press charges. I won't even tell anyone if you help me to a phone so I can call a cab."

Silence.

"I promise," she added. Her voice broke but a forced fought covered up the otherwise obvious display of emotion. A hot flash so powerful it made her dizzy swept up her spine. Elise tightened her grip on the bars and closed her eyes for a moment.

She took self-prescribed hormone replacement just like clockwork since she opted for a hysterectomy at 29, free of the burden of children and the embarrassment of stretch marks and a ruined body. Still, the heat built in her back and swarmed her extremities, coming to a peak at the crown of her head, which began to itch as if ants scrabbled across a peeling sunburn.

She couldn't help it. She scratched at it, coming away with a handful of perfectly weaved brunette hair stuck to slimy webbing between her fingers. She shoved her hand behind her back, stood up straight as she could, and backed up until her backside reached the wall.

The clown screamed and guffawed. Her scalp continued to itch and her guts burned so bad she bent at the waist, vomiting a neat pile onto the dirt. The clown didn't miss a beat, flat on his back, kicking wildly with the crazy red shoes clinging firmly to his feet.

"Get it off me!" he screamed.

No one saw what she'd done and Elise used the momentum borrowed from her waning dignity and kicked dirt over the spot of puke with what used to be an impeccably kept, scratch-free, Italian pump.

"Oh, my God." Whoever was responsible for her whereabouts was going to pay top dollar for a replacement pair, straight from Milan.

Evidence covered, she tried to stand up straight but her hips remained at an angle. She tried again and again, throwing her weight back. The result was the button launching off the waistband of her slacks and popping the melodramatic fucking clown in the temple.

"No! Don't shoot!" He squealed. "Haaa!" *Honk, honk.*

"Get a grip," Elise hissed through the bars. He didn't answer, just tore at the caked on makeup on his cheeks.

The button was the signal for her pants to give up the ghost in full and the waistband split, fabric falling away to her thighs. Her attempts to right herself made her feet scoot to and fro, and the resulting, piled up dirt berms chose that moment to fall over, covering her pumps with powdery soil. The inseams of her slacks split up the middle and her chest slammed against the flat of her naked thighs. She shoved back into the corner and hunched, losing both shoes and what was left of her pants. Cracked, red polish was the only thing reminiscent of her hands, if they could be called that. Clawed flippers remained. She hid them in the crook of her hips just as her ribcage popped where each rib met her spine, starting at the nape and ending with a solid crack in her lumbar. Her blouse screamed free, falling forward and dangling from each wrist as her torso widened in a quick explosion.

Elise bit back a whimper that pealed out through her nose in a shriek. The clown stopped scrubbing at his head to look at her.

"What?" she snapped with a thickened tongue. "And if you laugh I'll reach through these bars and put you out of your mystery, you freak of nature." The words came out slurred and rather botched, but his squinting eyes told her he got the gist.

"Promises, promises. And look who's talking," he sneered. "At least I can still speak." A small grin parted his blood red lips inside the painted grin and he broke into a series of laughing barks. "You've got a little something right here," he said, gesturing to the side of his face.

Elise felt her cheek, retrieving a matted hunk of hair with bits of scalp attached. There was no blood. Gingerly, she felt the top of her smooth head and temples. No sores marred her skin. The shape was new and much flatter, with flawless, tight and thick hide replacing cheekbones, eyebrows and her nose.

Panic expanded in her chest and the scream deflated into a gust of air. Elise opened her mouth, hoping it would release the bubble that grew in her trachea, but nothing came.

Screw it. She inhaled as much dust-riddled air as she could and screamed for her life. No sounds came. Instead, a loud, completely unladylike burp resounded against her palate and floated free through her nose. The sac beneath her jaws inflated against her chest. She closed her eyes.

"Croak."

"Perfect timing." The voice was familiar and hope sparked deep in her chest. She searched the dirt walk at the front of her cage for a rescue. Vic stepped into view. Elise cringed.

Salvation wasn't coming.

"Help!" she tried. The word merely hummed at the top of her mouth. Seeing Vic through narrowed lids, with watery depth, didn't change her perception of him much. But he was there with her and certainly able to help in some way. She stuck out an arm, the rags of what was a sensible but bulletproof workplace blouse waving, a white flag signaling her surrender.

Vic threw his head back, laughing viciously. Elise pulled her arm back, pulling the shredded material free of one wrist, or whatever she had instead, and then the other. If he stuck a hand through the bars she'd make a strong attempt at snapping it off at the elbow. She waited, glaring.

He wore a pinstriped suit and tie with a black derby. The dart gun protruded from one hand and the other grasped a mean looking whip. A radio crackled with static from his thick belt. Watching her cautiously, he holstered the whip in a loop by the radio and pulled a huge keyring forth, unlocking her cage. The skeleton key whizzed back on the retractable line, snapping into place beside the others beneath his coat.

"You will hold still," he said, swinging the cage door

open. He waved the gun in warning.

Elise crouched low, trying to be small but her shoulder stood as tall as his waist. Vic hurried forth, dart at the ready, and slipped a thick collar around her neck. She threw her head from side to side, clawing at it with her front flippers. She tried to stand and back away but her thickly muscled legs overcompensated, sending her into the side of the cage. She recovered quickly and backed into the corner again, near hyperventilation.

"Time to see the kiddies," he said. The leash came taught, jerking the collar against her jaw. She leaned forward, one shaky, webbed foot in front of the other, and waddled after him.

Music grew louder and deepened the sickness balled in her gut. Overhead lights grew impossibly bright, making it hard for her to see. She stumbled but was jerked back into place by Vic and his relentless leash. They traveled a dirt walk with black iron bars at the sides while her eyes watered, collecting dust. Hoards of people, families with young children, and strolling couples stood before tents. The spinning top of a carousel came into view, slowing as they neared. Vic pulled a gate open and drug Elise toward a wide set of steps leading up to a wooden platform. The clown was on all fours, a thick metal band around his waste. The metal held him straight, his back a flat platform with a padded seat saddling his shoulders.

"Ha ha!" he screamed.

"Up with you," Vic said, dragging Elise toward a vacant spot between the clown and a huge, brown and black spider. As she neared, the arachnid tapped nervously with its front legs. A similar seat was bolted around the spider's midsection. Vic pulled her head close to a pole that ran from the floor up under the tented carousel top, and strapped the leash tight. A carny pulled her into line with the others and secured a pad to her back with irons.

"Good to go!" yelled the carny. The ride began to spin, a line of small, squealing children waiting behind a latched entry. A neon sign hung between two gate posts. The lettering was backward from her vantage but as the carny strapped squirming kids to each abomination's padded seat, and the carousel spun to pick up new passengers, Elise was able to read the name of the ride:

LOATHSOME CREATURES

THE BLOODIEST SHOW ON EARTH

ADAM MILLARD

The convoy pulled onto the barren field just before 4:00 pm. Ten vehicles, all towing trailers, slowed as they reached the center of the clearing. The trailers were covered with mucky tarpaulins, though various structures poked out through the rain-drenched material; multicolored stalagmites of steel and electrics that, when lit up, would draw everybody in the village.

The van at the front of the convoy shut down. A man climbed out, as tall as he was broad and had the appearance of a professional wrestler. His long, black trenchcoat concealed the hulking figure beneath. He made a gesture, a circling motion with one gigantic hand, to the other vehicles, and they circled around him.

He scanned the field, the houses, and farms at the far side, and knew that they had made a good choice. Population 500, a small society that had probably never witnessed the magic of a traveling show. There would be complaints in the hours to follow, but only from a minority believing the convoy to be gypsies rolling into town with the sole purpose of destroying the field before moving on to the next. It was expected, and therefore boring. He had no time for such idiots. He came to give the majority what they wanted, something they never saw before.

A show they would never forget.

"Kane," a voice said. He turned to find Angela, beautiful Angela, the star of the show, and his most prized possession. "I've told the others to begin setting up. Do you need me for anything?"

Kane thought about it. There were a few good hours before showtime, and he knew what he wanted to do to Angela, but instead shook his head. "You may get some rest," he told her. "Tonight is going to be explosive. I can feel it."

Angela could, too. Kane knew that her teeth would already buzzing, an excitement that she could neither control nor conceal. They all loved these hours, the calm before the storm. The rain hammering down all around would no doubt put a few people off attending, but there would be plenty of others, arriving in time to see the magnificence, the splendor, the downright lunacy of the unraveling chaos.

"Send Ives and Tre into the village," Kane grunted. "Tell them I want posters on every fucking thing a poster will stick to."

Angela grinned. "It's going to be a good night?"

He nodded. "One that none of us will forget in a hurry."

Within an hour everybody knew about the show. The news traveled so fast that people from the next town over,

Perton, had already arrived to see what all the fuss was about.

An irate priest ranted outside the village-hall. "*We don't want this in our village. They're nothing but a bunch of vagabonds, looters and thieves.*" He soon realized that nobody paid him any mind and gave up. He cursed under his breath and disappeared into the hall, quickly making the sign of the cross afterward...just in case.

Children excitedly ran through the street, knocking on the doors of those not yet in the know. Their parents were either present in the street, or not bothered in the slightest regarding their offsprings' sudden disappearance. In truth, the village had never known such palpable excitement. Everything was a buzz. It was as if the village had been treated to an early Christmas. Sure, the cynics were out in force, demeaning the traveling show and its "*no doubt in-bred*" workforce. The children didn't care. You could have told them that AIDS had just pulled onto the adjacent field and they would have *still* gone to watch.

The strange little men that hung posters in the street were swamped with questions, and they kept exchanging glances, unsure of what they were allowed to say, and what was to remain a secret.

One disheveled, ginger-haired child asked, "Is there gonna be a freak show?" His face was peppered with freckles to the extent that he appeared to have a very nice tan for the time of year.

"Oh, *yes*," the man with the hammer said. He had teeth that looked like a row of popcorn, and he dribbled as he spoke. "The freakiest, most disgusting-est freak show of all time."

This clearly ruffled the young urchin's feathers because, without warning, he leapt three feet into the air, punching at nothing with his fist. "*Yes*! I bet there's an alligator-man, or a woman with a *beard*. Mister, is there a–"

The man holding the nail growled. The ginger-haired child stopped talking. In fact, he looked downright terrified. "He said, 'wait and see,'" he grunted. "So why don't you do us a favor and go pester somebody else?"

The child brightened, as if he hadn't just been reproached for his annoying behavior. He turned and raced off down the street, disappearing into an alleyway. They could hear him singing, a tuneless little ditty neither of the men recognized, as he went. The workers would be crooning it in their own heads for most of the evening.

There was one pub in the village, a quaint but busy place called The Duck With Two Heads. The villagers simply referred to it as The Duck. Standing outside, a group of retired men prattled on about the sudden encroachment and watched the mayhem unfold.

"This would have never happened in my day," one of them said, sucking hard on a pipe that had long been extinguished. "It's *appalling*. They just *roll* up, in the middle of a Sunday afternoon, and expect people to swoon over them, treat them like celebrities. They're a pissing *nuisance* is what they are, and I will be writing a strongly-worded letter to the council."

The two men standing with him nodded, silently approving his intentions. One of them, an ex-paratrooper by the name of William Cotton, rubbed his fist into the palm of his hand. "In my day we fought people like that," he said. "I'd love to have a bout with the bloke in charge. Reckon I'd knock the living shit out of him."

And so the three men discussed exactly what they would do to the ringmaster, should they ever meet. It was decided that a boycott of the event was the next best thing, and they went about plotting the downfall of that evening's show like the three deluded, over-the-hill patriots they were.

Not fifty feet away, shackled in a basement, lay the daughter of two very strict disciplinarians. Emily Swain knew how to remove the chains, though; she'd had plenty of time to learn over the years. She had even, on occasion, slept through the whole ordeal, ignoring the restraints and drifting off into alternate realms. Right now she couldn't sleep. Something was going on outside, something that she felt she was missing out on. A child was screaming at the top of his voice about some bearded lady, and another excitedly begged his mother to take him somewhere later on.

Emily pushed herself up on the bed, her chains rattling noisily again the rails behind her. Her left arm had gone to sleep, and she repeatedly opened and shut her fist in an attempt to alleviate the torturous pins and needles in her hand. Upstairs her mother stamped across the landing, no doubt preparing tea. Emily loathed her. Not for continually locking her in the basement as a punishment against general mischievousness, but for her complete indifference about doing so as if it were the most normal thing in the world to chain a little girl up in a dank, dripping, putrid basement. She hated her father, but only because he hadn't the gumption or the courage to step in. Emily saw the glances he shot her as Victoria tightened the chains; apologetic, remorseful, but he lacked the temerity to say something. In a way, she felt sorry for him, just as he did for her. Victoria was a callous, horrific example of a human. Her comeuppance was long overdue.

Emily could stand it no longer, and wriggled over onto her side. In the wall behind her there was a pin, the key to her freedom. She reached back and removed a little of the crumbled concrete from a crevice. She was always very careful at the next part; dropping the pin would leave her bound to the bed, and the pin would be exposed, waiting on the floor next to the bed for her mother to discover.

She plucked it up between thumb and forefinger, breathing gently, and began to work at the lock. She had done it a hundred times, usually just so she could walk around the basement until the pain from lying motionless for so long dissipated. It was simple, and within ten seconds she was shuffling loose of the chains and stretching her legs over the side of the bed.

There was a bang upstairs, then sounds of her mother reprimanding somebody in the street as she told them to act their age and not their shoe-size. Another bang, then silence.

Emily looked up to the small, rectangular window. It wasn't much bigger than her now. A few more months and she wouldn't be able to fit through. She would have to stay in the basement. With no chance of sneaking out – like she was about to now.

Perhaps, she thought, that bitch of a mother might realize the error of her ways; treat her more like the young lady she was becoming and not like some sort of animal that needed to be restrained every time a mistake was made. It was the human equivalent of having her nose rubbed in piss, though she guessed even an animal would eventually learn from its errors.

She pulled the crate across – heavy, filled with old newspapers that her father refused to discard like any normal person – and stepped up onto it. Rain poured outside and she was hardly dressed for trawling the streets. Her thin, white dress did little to protect her from the elements, and her mother would know that she had somehow managed to escape from her drenched clothes. Emily began to have second thoughts about the whole thing.

Damn rain.

And then she pushed the latch across, heaved the

window open, and climbed out into the already darkening street.

What the hell, she thought.

The main structures were up, leaving just a few tents and stalls to erect. At the edge of the milieu, a fat clown blew up balloons with a hand-pump. From the expression on his face he was not the happiest clown in the world. A woman, slender and beautiful, walked by him, smiling. She was a contortionist, able to fit into a box two feet square. "Come on, only a hundred more to go," she said. The clown gave her the finger and growled, to which she suddenly quickened her pace.

A man wearing a fox mask walked, somewhat unsteadily, on eight-foot stilts, practicing for the upcoming performance. Tonight he planned to attempt a trampoline back-flip, something that he had only managed to complete once.

The regular line-up of freaks took to their booths in the large tent adjacent to the main structure. Bearded-lady, Two-faced-Jack – though the second face was merely a birth defect resulting in an unsightly protrusion no larger than a carbuncle, Jess The Painted Lady – who had more tattoos than she had skin, and The Coat-hanger Kid, a boy with the rather gruesome ability of being able to push a whole coat-hanger into his mouth, resulting in one of the most evil grins imaginable. They filed through into their respective booths, concealed behind large purple curtains until showtime. The air was buzzing with anticipation. It always was this close to the performance.

In his own personal tent, Kane smeared paint across his face. With no mirror in front of him, he smudged blacks and browns over his cheeks and forehead. With that done, he wiped his darkened fingers on a rag and made his way out into the semi-darkness of the night.

"Ladies, gentlemen, and children," the large man with the painted face screamed towards the audience. "I'm glad you decided to join us on this, our most *anticipated* night. We have a show for you the likes of which you will have *never* seen."

"You shouldn't *be* here!" an old man in the crowd yelled. Heads snapped across in his direction; children began to boo and hiss at the interrupter, who retook his seat, perturbed but not beaten. "Shouldn't be here," he muttered as an aside.

"I, your lowly host, *Kane*, can only apologize for such short-notice. We are a traveling show, and where we lay our hat we play." The man with the smeared face bowed. Women in the audience – mothers, sisters, adolescent girls who were yet to discover true feelings – audibly swooned.

"To begin with," Kane continued, straightening up from his courteous gesture, "I give you...." A drum-roll thundered from off-stage, working the audience up into a frenzy. "Poker the Clown." He moved across the center of the tent, making way for the entertainer's big entrance, which appeared to involve running headlong into the main tent-support. The crowd erupted with laughter and the clown scrambled to his feet, shaking his head for comedic effect.

Kane grinned, knowing the time was almost upon them.

Emily was soaked to the bone by the time she reached the field. Her dress clung to her, accentuating every curve of her body. Her long, dark hair clung to her forehead, and she pulled it across, tucking it behind her ears, so she could see what she was looking at.

It was magnificent. So many beautiful lights, flickering and dancing, illuminating the entire field. Emily felt her heart leap in her chest, excitement that she had never felt before. She crossed the deserted field – everybody was inside the main tent, judging from the rapturous noise emanating from within – and began to search for a way in, one that didn't cost her anything. At the rear of the main tent was an entrance, though she guessed it was for performers only. After a quick check she saw nobody and made her way through, out of the steadily drumming rain and into the mouth of the dragon.

There had to be somewhere she could hunker down, watch the show for free without being discovered. It was getting late, and Emily's mother would have probably already discovered her absence from the basement. She was in for it when she returned, but right now that didn't matter. What mattered was getting a good view of the show.

She could hear the screaming, happy noises on the opposite side of the canvas. There was no door leading to the main arena, and so Emily dropped to her knees and began to scoop at the mud beneath the tent. Thankfully the rain had softened the ground, and it was relatively easy work. She lay flat on her belly – ignoring the fact that her dress was completely ruined, covered with brown sludge – and dragged herself down into the small hole. There were feet in front of her, and chairs, but most importantly she saw the clown buffoonery directly ahead, providing the man in the chair remained still, she had a perfect view. She smiled, happy that she had made the right decision.

To hell with the circumstances.

The audience ate up the acts as they performed. Isabella the Contortionist was particularly popular with the male contingency, provoking wolf-whistles and excited hoots as she climbed, somewhat erotically, into the tiny box in the center of the stage. The three elderly men sitting together near the back were not impressed, however, and shouted obscenities at the "Female Devil Whore" as she emerged from her case to vociferous applause. The geriatric gents glanced around the room, tutting as loud as they could at the enchanted crowd, but it was no good. People were just having too much of a good time, and refused to have it spoiled by a trio of fuddy-duddy old fuckers.

Between acts, the colossal man with the painted face returned to whip the crowd up, ready for the next performance. A stilt-walking fox, a tightrope walking woman in a tight, red catsuit – she looked as if she had been stitched into it, such was its constraint – and a knife-throwing midget who, despite his size, didn't miss one, single balloon. The audience loved every minute of it, and so did the little girl hiding just out of sight beneath their feet.

Emily clapped along, breathlessly mesmerized by what she witnessed. Her mother would be waiting for her, right now, at home, pissed off beyond anything she could possibly imagine, and yet she didn't care, for now she was having so much fun, and the memory of it would last her a lifetime.

It was worth a thousand hours in the basement.

A *million*.

"Ladies and gentlemen, boys and girls," the herculean ringmaster sighed as he once again took center-stage. "You have been amazing for us on this wondrous night. Would you please, one last time, as loud as possible, show some love for all our acts."

The audience applauded. Three very annoyed old men got up and began to shuffle down the row towards the exit.

"But, *alas*, our time is up, and I'm afraid that we must move along." The man glanced towards the side of the tent. A beautiful woman appeared, nodded at him, and zipped up the canvas from the inside. "And can I ask you all to please make your way out of the tent in an orderly fashion, as a stampede would no doubt kill every single one of you and make our job a lot easier." He laughed, some kind of sick joke that nobody in the crowd understood. People muttered, filling the awkward silence that descended beneath the canvas roof. The old men stopped moving, and nodded to each other, as if their assumptions had been correct all along.

A few people in the audience began to jeer, as if the joke had tainted their otherwise amazing evening, though the expression on the ringmaster's face didn't change...at least for a few seconds.

Then his neck snapped as if it had been broken by an invisible hand. His head rolled back on its loose pivot, and he began to grunt as if the pain was too much to bear. The audience fell silent, intrigued by what was happening to the man in the center ring. Perhaps it was another trick, something to cap off the night in style. He dropped to his knees; there was an audible crack as his legs bent back in an unnatural manner. The ringmaster tore at his golden shirt with both hands, ripping it away from his skin with sharpened nails.

The three miserable men amongst the crowd tried to push forward, but everybody was standing still, rapt by this latest trickery. The woman who entered a few seconds before joined in, rolling around on the muddy ground and tearing at herself. Elsewhere on the site, others screamed, grunted, *growled*

A man said, "This is absolutely absurd!" and plucked his son up and carried him, under one arm like a beach-towel, toward the exit. "This was meant to be a *family-show*, was it not?"

He expected a response from the ringmaster – or for him to suddenly straighten up and apologize. He would be waiting for a while. No one played any sort of game. What was happening to him, to *all* of them, was real. Fighting it was pointless, and why would they even *want* to?

All of a sudden, from the side of the ring, the fox on stilts rushed forward. The crowd gasped as he lunged, dropped eight-feet to the ground – with his hind legs still tethered to the stilts – and landed on outstretched arms. His hands were no longer human. They seemed to have swollen and extended. The mask that previously sat flush to his face was now pushed away, a genuine snout protruding underneath the plastic one.

Finally people started to panic. Women screamed, ushering upset children toward the exits, away from the maniacs in the middle of the tent, as far away as possible. A few men, burly-looking fellows, stepped forward, a sign of either bravery or stupidity. Time would tell on that one. They watched as the ringmaster arched his back, previously naked flesh sprouting fine, silver fur. When he looked up with a mouth contorted in pain, his eyes were solid white. Tiny red pin-pricks appeared at the center of the orbs, then the man's face exploded outwards, stretching twice as long in less than a second.

Burly men recoiled at the sudden change. They offered each other cursory glances, yet maintained the bare-knuckle stances that they stood in.

"Get everyone out of here!" a man cried from the side of the tent. A second later his head flew through the air, thumped against the side of a generator and landed in the mud. After that, all hell broke loose. The acts were nowhere to be seen. In their place, hairy, bipedal demons circled the audience, growling and slavering over their prey.

A woman wearing a beautiful yellow dress ran for the exit. She almost made it before the clown – hairier now, but still recognizable from the color of the face-paint tipping its fur – lunged for her. In one quick, erratic movement it clawed through her dress. The woman fell silent, realizing something was wrong. She looked down – her insides were hollow and blood squirted out in a fine, arterial spray. She dropped onto her back, eyes rolling like the worst comedy-faint ever.

The fox-demon was still attached to its stilts, and therefore unable to drag itself closer to the screaming crowd in any hurry. The mask popped off as the elastic finally snapped. Beneath was something much more horrific. It opened its maws, trying to snap at any ankle close enough to bite. Then it howled, calling for help, struggling slowly forward through the mud- and blood-soaked arena.

Two men tried to keep the ringmaster away using overturned chairs. The creature lashed out, swiping at the wooden legs pointing towards it. There was a crunch before three of the legs splintered and shot across the room. One of them plunged into a fat lady's face, and her impossibly shrill screaming became even more intense as she realized she had a chair-leg in her head. She staggered for the exit, slipped on the mud, and landed facedown. The wooden leg shot out through her graying hair, a pink blob of brain on its tip.

The second man crashed his chair against the creature, but it simply shattered, useless. The ringmaster growled, reached out, and latched onto the man's head. It twisted, and the head came right off, the tendril that was the man's spinal-cord hung down and flapped around like a rat's tail.

Stepping back, the first man hoped to put some distance between himself and this demonic creature. He realized that he still held the chair-seat; its single leg jutting out like a wooden phallus. Tossing it aside, he turned. Something grab his ankle. He looked down. A creature – smaller than the ringmaster – pulled itself out of a box, using him as leverage.

Isabella the Contortionist, snapping as thick, viscous drool seeped from her frothing mouth, lunged for him. He opened his mouth to scream, but nothing came out. He didn't have time. The creature was out of its box, wrapped around his leg and snapped at his groin with razor-sharp teeth. He toppled backwards, landing with a thump in the mud. He felt the thing climbing up his body, claws digging into him, tearing flesh away. And then there was agony. He glanced down and, through blurred vision, witnessed his entrails leaving his body, the hairy little contortionist forcing them into her mouth, sucking them up like spaghetti.

Death came seconds later; and not a moment too soon.

People were crushed up against the side of the tent, searching for a door to release them from this insanity. There was an almighty howl from across the field. Some people managed to escape, to break out into the night, but they had not imagined the terror that would be waiting for them.

Two children ran to the edge of the clearing, sobbing and panting. Had they just seen their father torn in half by a tattooed werewolf? Surely not. Things like this didn't happen in real life.

"David! Are we going to *die*?" the little girl asked her brother. Her blood-soaked pigtails slapped her around the face as she ran.

"I don't know," he panted. Then something attacked him from behind, sending him sprawling into the mud. His sister screamed as the beast ripped David apart. It was the clown. She saw, even in the darkness of the night, the white powdered make-up flaking away from its fur. She stood and began to run, hoping her jellied legs would carry her across the field. Behind her, the creature snarled as it fed. Parts of David were flung aside, perhaps for later, and when it was finished with her brother, it turned and lunged towards the little girl, who had separated herself from the creature by less than twenty feet. She managed an almost inaudible squeak as the full weight of the beast landed on top of her. And she remembered no more.

Members of what was, only a few moments ago, a very happy audience – were racing away from the tent, only to be picked off by snarling beasts. From the outside, the canvas looked darker than it had, thanks to the blood painting the interior. Lights from the exterior attractions continued to flash and flicker, though the crowd no longer marveled at them.

Emily pulled herself forward, still out of sight. This couldn't be happening. She thought about her mother, about the basement, about her father and how he stood off when she needed him the most. All of those things ran through her head, and yet true horror stared her right in the face. There was a body, decapitated, lying a few feet in front of her. The necklace hanging around the bloodied stump of its neck was instantly recognizable. Juliette Gower, one of the tutors at the school she attended. She knew this because she had dreamed of owning such a beautiful piece of jewelery. Staring at it now, though, she saw the small nuggets of flesh sticking to it, and found it lost its appeal.

Dragging herself slowly forward, slipping and sliding through the blood and mud, she managed to climb to her feet. An arm flew past her face, so close she saw the cuff-link on its still-sleeved wrist. Something growled behind her, and she span to find the silver-furred creature prowling towards her, slavering.

Emily grabbed for the nearest thing available – a crystal ball, blood-spattered and smeared with viscera – and threw it, as hard as she could, towards the approaching beast. It connected with the creature's jaw. It howled, shook its head, and spat a tooth out onto the ground. Emily knew, in that instant, that she was going to die. Her legs turned to jelly as she tried to run. The creature landed on her back, pushing her face-down into the gory mire beneath. She dragged herself forward beneath the bleacher, but the creature's frenzied attack was too much, its weight too immense.

The last thing she heard was a hellish chorus, a unison of howls that signaled the end of a village.

The tents came down at first light. They were scrubbed haphazardly to remove the majority of the blood and gore, before loading onto the vehicles. It would be a month before another show like that, plenty of time to give the tents a thorough hosing. In the meantime they would lay low, rehearse new tricks, and enjoy life. They were, for now, sated.

Kane asked, "We almost ready to roll?" Ives and Tre stood to attention, and looked almost comical in doing so.

"About ten more minutes," Tre said. "It'll be like we were never here."

"Apart from that," Ives added, pointing to the huge mound of bodies at the edge of the field. "Lot of leftovers this time, don't you think? Maybe we should bury them."

Kane shook his head. "Fuck them," he grunted. "We don't have time."

He headed across to his van and began to unfold a map. He traced a route with one jagged fingernail, and had almost planned the next journey when the map was suddenly snatched out of his hands.

A small girl stood in front of him. She looked annoyed, petulant, like she could be a real handful if she wanted to be. Kane didn't recognize her, which meant that she was one of the villagers.

But she wasn't running away.

"I want a *word* with you," the girl said, spinning round and pulling her dress up at the back. There were claw-marks from the nape of her neck to the small of her back. The wound was already healing. By tomorrow it would be nothing more than a pretty white scar. She turned back to the hulking man, a look on her face that suggested he'd better explain himself, and quickly.

He rolled his eyes and sighed. "Have you got any tricks?" he asked her.

She smiled. "I can roll my tongue," she said, excitedly. "And I can do *this*." She did a handstand, followed by a cartwheel, and almost ended up face-down in the mud. She straightened up and awaited his appraisal.

"I suppose that'll have to do," he said. "Get in the

van...what's your name?"

She grinned, suddenly devoid of all innocence. The child inside her had already died. "Emily," she said. She climbed into the van and watched the rest of the performers load up. A few minutes later and they were pulling away from the field...away from the pile of mutilated bodies and heading towards somewhere new; a place where they would put on another show. A better show. An even bloodier show.

The bloodiest show on earth.

WITHIN THREE POUNDS

PATRICK FLANAGAN

"Winner every day here," he said into the microphone. "Winner every hour.

"Who's it gonna be?

"You, sir? Right there, in the ten-gallon hat and the ten dollar boots. Come on up. Come on, don't be shy. Sir…what's your name, sir?"

"Jules."

"Jules? Really?" A few chuckles from the onlookers.

"Yeah, that's right."

"I gotta tell you, you don't look like a Jules." More polite laughter. It was early in the day, and the booth had only attracted a handful of spectators so far, maybe a baker's dozen in all. "Maybe it's the spurs. Anyway, Cowboy Jules, come on over here, center stage, so everyone can get a good look at you. You're lookin' lean and mean, Jules. Leathery. Like an empty saddlebag. Now, Jules, I can guess your weight within three pounds…well, you read the sign, right? I'm off by more than three pounds either way, you get your prize, an' if I call it…." He slid

67

the crowd a grin from out of the corner of his mouth. The ring toss, the milk cans, the pitcher's mound all promised more excitement—and seemingly better odds of winning. But he was warming up now, getting a feel for today's crowd. Every day was different. "And I will call it…well, you get a big ol' bag of diddly. But you have fun either way, right?

"So come on over and let me size you up.

"Uh *huh*. Jules, I'm here to tell you that you weigh in at a hundred and sixty-three pounds." The acne-scarred kid behind the counter reached over and smacked the bell with the little rubber hammer. CLANG! "That's right, one-sixer-three. Now climb aboard the S.S. *Moment of Truth* here and we'll see what we'll see…."

The kid reached down and flicked the slide whistle switch behind the counter. "Winner every day, winner every day…." The oversized scale needle spun theatrically as Cowboy Jules stepped up onto the platform scale. "And my-oh-my, what have we here? Looks like…a hundred and sixty-one and a half pounds of grade-A cowpoke, that's what! Well, yee-*haw*, Jules." The kid flicked the Loser's Anthem toggle switch. *Wah-wah-wah-waaaahhhh.* "Now, Julie, I happen to like cowboys…not in a Brokeback sorta way, don't worry…but you been a good sport, and you're my first victim of the day, so here you go. Parting gift, like they used to say on the game shows." He took the stuffed animal the kid held out for him, a little green elephant with cheap stitching, and handed it to Jules. The cowboy smiled sheepishly. "There ya go. *Vaya con dios, amigo.* That's it, down the steps and around the back, if you please. Let's everybody give Cowboy Jules a hand for bein' such a sport. Now, who's it gonna be?

"There's a winner every day here, winner *every* day. So who's it gonna be?"

Not too far off, across the gravel-dusted clearing, he

could hear the grinding squeal of the Round-Up as it rose into the air over the carnival, just barely holding together from the sound of it. Kids walking past the booth were laughing; parents were scolding them to stay close, to finish their cotton candy, to stop fighting, to take *that* out of their mouth, this instant, who knows where that had been, put that down *now*, honey. Grandparents on balloon and stuffed animal duty trudged behind, trying to keep up with the young folks. The carnival was fully awake by now, shaking off the dust and the dewdrops of a chilly August morning and laying out under the warm midday sun.

And the crowd around his booth had steadily grown to a nice size now, a little over twenty. Some of them were bored and just wanted a show. And some of them knew—just *knew*—they could beat him. Beat the pants off him.

His grin was an honest one. He loved his job, and he was ready for them. Bring 'em on.

"Who's gonna show me up here, in front of all these people? Come on, now. You, sir? No? All right.

"How about you, miss? Yes, you, with the balloons. No? Okay, well don't you float *too* far away from me, now. Pretty girls always bring me luck. How about you, young feller? No? All right.

"Well now. Here we go. Here. We. *Go!* You seem pretty confident, my friend. *Pretty*…darn…confident. Now why don't you come on over here and let me check out the goods.

"Well, now.

"Well, well, well. See, my new friend here wore himself a long, heavy coat. How's that July sunshine treating you, friend? Why don't you hang your coat up and stay for a while? C'mon…that's it.

"Now, I wouldn't say you're *heavy*, exactly." He paused for the zinger. "Wouldn't *say* it…now, now, just joshin'

69

you, buddy, never fear," he added, sympathetically shushing the old lady in the front of the crowd braying like a mule. "This is all in good fun and you're a heck of a sport. So let's do this. Not really heavy but not really skinny. On the short side, just like me. Older guy, *not* like me. I, of course, am twenty-seven years old." He looked sharply at the laughing crowd. "Hell, it ain't *that* funny, guys. All right, all right, so maybe that's not exactly, precisely my age. Let's call it Twenty-seven *Plus*. For the both of us.

"When you get to be twenty-seven plus, your body kinda…settles in, you know. See, this is the craft here, folks. This is the art. I see you and I see through the abandoned diets, the drinking…the pounds you put on after you quit smoking, the pounds you *dropped* when you thought maybe the boss might come in unexpectedly one day, am I right?" Some theatrical boos from the back of the crowd. (Definitely more than thirty now.)

"When he came in five minutes after you snuck your girlfriend out the back door, and you just *knew* that *he* knew what was going on? Don't be coy, now.

"When you thought he might decide to count the safe out with you, before you had a chance to put back what you borrowed, yeah? Am I right?

"Thoughts like those just *sweat* those Twinkies and those late-night pizza fries right out of your pores, friend.

"Believe me, I know.

"I've been doing this for, heck…Twenty-*six* Plus years, heh…and you get a feel for these things, if you follow me. Hey, I *like* you, pardner. What's your name?

"…don't wanna divulge, huh? Alright, alright, fair enough, but I gotta call you *somethin'*, can't just say 'Hey you.' Tell you what, in show business you get a stage name, so that's what I'll give you. You're Sam. Everybody say 'Hi, Sam.'"

"*Hi, Sam!*" most of the crowd chimed back, some of

them laughing at their own awkwardness. Two carnies stood off to one side, hands shoved in pockets. Hand-rolled cigarettes dangled from their lips. By now, there'd been a complete turnover from Jules' crowd, and he could tell that most of these newcomers were just gawkers. He had something a pattern. He'd call on four or five gawk-ers and goad and tease them to give it a try; most of them were shy, but every so often one of them would be a sport and step right up. He enjoyed making the other kind of spectator…the ones with just a glint of desperation in their eyes…wait. Because they *would* wait.

"All right, Sam, now I saw you watching from the bench over there in front of Judy's Fro-yo Jamboree dur-ing Cowboy Jules' rodeo, so you know the rules. I guess your weight within three pounds…and trust me, I *will* guess it…or you get yourself a prize. And Sam, I'm here to tell you that you weigh…"

He drew the moment out for the crowd.

"One hundred…and…ninety-seven pounds."
CLANG! "Now, are we all ready?"

The crowd answered that yes, it sure was ready.

"And Sammy boy, are *you* ready?"

Sam said nothing, but nodded that yes, he was ready. One of the carnies muttered something to the other, who chuckled and shook his head.

"O-kay! Now just step on up here, and—" As Sam walked past the railing, a loud squeal echoed across the covered booth. *oooohWEEEooooh.* "Whoa! Hold on there, friend. Hang on just a second." He didn't have to look to see the carnies already making their way through the crowd.

"Hang on just a moment…Sam, can I ask you to take two steps directly backwards, please.

"Well, I'm asking. But I don't have to."

The carny at Sam's side didn't say anything. Just leaned

against the railing and rested his hand on the straight peen hammer slung low on his hip. Sam held the back of his left hand. He glanced down at the hammer, and the glance became a stare.

"That's right."

The second squeal was just as loud. "Well, well, well. Sammy! Sammy, what can I say here. Folks, I know, I know…it's cynical. And it's mistrusting. And it says a heck of a lot about my outlook on life, and I agree with you all a thousand percent, except for when folks like Sam come here and set off my metal detectors. Sam, I'm gonna have to ask you to kick off your sneakers, please. You can have them back after you ride the scale…

"Thank you, Sam. Buck up, friend. This is just a game, am I right?"

He took the sneakers from where Sam had kicked them across the stage. "Folks, I'd like to show you something. Our friend Samuel here is famous. Did you know that?" He nodded sagely.

"You may even have seen him on your TV set. True story.

"When he's not visiting our lovely park, Sam works as a Budweiser Clydesdale." He held up Sam's shoes, turning them around so the crowd could see the metal soles. He tapped them against the railing so everyone could hear the clang. "Another one of those little tricks you pick up, after you've been doing this for Twenty-six Plus years. Now, you don't often find sneakers with metal soles, do you, Sam?"

Sam said nothing.

"Well, Sam's not feeling too talkative, so I'll answer. No, you don't. And see that, right there? That seam? That's where Sam glued the boot soles onto the bottom of the sneaker, thinking he could steal a march on Yours Truly." He looked at Sam and flashed his pearlies.

"It was a nice try, friend. But now that you're a little lighter in the loafers, climb on board and we'll see what we see. Winner every day here, folks. Winner every hour."

The slide whistle dipped and rose, soon followed by the Loser's Anthem.

"And...that's right, you guessed it folks. One hundred and ninety-five. There we go! Thank you, Sam! Here's your horseshoes back! You have yourself a *swell* day. Folks, let's all give Sam a hand for playing." The crowd clapped dutifully. "Damon, Keith, why don't you give Sam here a hand with his shoes, around back. He might need help tying those laces up tight. Bye, Sam. Who's it gonna be?

"Who's next now?

"Winner every *day*, every *hour*...heck, practically every *minute* here. Who's next?

"Sir? No? Well, okay, you have a good one.

"How about you, ma'am? All right, step on up. Come on, folks, you can clap louder than that, let's hear it. What's your name, ma'am?

"I'm sorry, could you just speak into the microphone, just a little more loudly, dear."

"Claudia."

"Well, hi there, Claudia. And you know, we don't do ages her, no we don't. Weight's dangerous enough, but guessing age? Hell, that's how I lost these two teeth right here." Another donkey bray. "But if you'll indulge me, please, Claudia dear...I'm looking at you, and I kind of have a feel for this, you know, and I'm gonna say you are...thirty-five years old."

Claudia smiled and waved him off. Oh, go on, such *things* you say. "You're off by about fifteen years," she said, laughing hoarsely.

"Go on. Really? There's no way. *No* way. Well...maybe I oughtta stick to what I know best, then. Now come on up, Claudia, and let us all have a look. I'm gonna ask the gentlemen in the audience not to cat-call, please. Let's keep it clean. Come on over here, dear. Johnny, hold the lady's purse, please.

"Well now, you're a healthy-looking woman, Claudia. I mean no disrespect, certainly. That's a compliment in my book. Healthy and hale, indeed. But I have to ask after your paleness. Are you feeling all right, sweetheart?" Claudia nodded that she felt just fine—a little too quickly, a little too emphatically. "Particularly with this hot summer sun. We don't want anyone passing out. Are you sure you're fine?"

"*Yes*," Claudia said.

"Not feeling dizzy?"

"No, no," Claudia said, "no, not at all."

"I imagine the heat's positively stifling for you, what with that long-sleeved blouse you're wearing. Why don't you roll those up for us, set our minds at ease?" Claudia looked at the crowd hesitantly, hoping for some support, but there didn't seem to be any white knights standing in attendance. "Keith, why don't you lend Claudia a hand…"

"E-excuse *me*! Take your, *no*, take your…take your hands off…" Her voice trailed away as Keith squeezed his grip hard; she barked out one sharp whimper, then remained silent.

"Miss Claudia. If you'll pardon my saying so, you seem somewhat worse for wear. These marks here, all up your arms. Like little bruises. Folks, can you all see what I'm looking at here?" Claudia tried to cross her arms, but Keith twisted again and she let her arms go limp. "Yep, there…there…there, and there…looks like *some*body left the fairgrounds, which as y'all know we strenuously recommend you *not* do, and went wading along the lakefront. Wanted to pet yourself a catfish, sweetheart, was that it? I'll bet that was it. See, folks, this is Exhibit A for why we gotta post signs like that in the first place. Claudia, let's show all the…Keith, if you could—thank you kindly, Keith. See, there's all manner o' critters in that lake. You got cottonmouths, you got your snappin' turtles, and you got *leeches*. God *damn*, I hate leeches.

"What'd they take out of those tired old veins, Claudia, half a pint? Maybe more?

"Anything for that edge, right? Take *juuuuust* enough out of you to beat the spread. Well, dear, you can fool everybody sometimes, and some people all the time, and some people no time at all."

He smiled, and leaned in close, holding the microphone a kiss away from his lips.

"And guess which kind of fella *I* am." Boos, cackles, some scattered claps.

"I'm a fella who says that you…are…one hundred…and…thirty…*two*. One-thirty-two, folks. I'm calling it."

CLANG!

"Now, step up on the scales of justice here. Go on.

"Let's hear that sweet music!"

Wah-wah-wah-waaaahhhh. More clapping.

"Looky, looky. That's what they call a bull's eye, sweetheart. One hundred and thirty-two, on the proverbial nose. Sorry, dear! No prize for you! No draught of victory's sweet nectar! Just a short ride on a short bus, back to Loserville, population you and twelve cats!" A few men in the back laughed sharply. "You can step down now, sugar tits, go on. Keith, help Miss Claudia down. Everybody, let's have a round of applause for Miss Claudia!

"That's it, right on around the back, Keith. Usual spot. Thanks."

Murmurs and nervous giggles began to make their way to the platform from the back of the crowd. "Whoa now! Looks like we've got ourselves a VIP there in the back! Make way, kids, make way." People dutifully shuffled to one side as a six-feet-tall anthropomorphic rodent wearing a bright purple bowler hat and matching vest and tie came shambling toward the stage. The children in the crowd smiled and laughed loudly. The adults seemed less jubilant. One crossed herself as the creature brushed against her as it passed.

"Look who it is, *Mister* Victor Vole himself! Heya, Vic. Gimme four." The vole slapped a huge, floppy, white-gloved paw across his outstretched hand. "All right! Vic, you here to test your wits against the All-Powerful, Indisputable Scale?"

Laughter from the kids. "No? Well why not, Vic? Didn't you see how much fun these people have been having? Isn't that right, folks?

"Not brave enough, that it? I see. So you're just here to get in my way, that it, Vic? Well, why don't you just scoot on off to one side and let through *our next volunteer*! You, sir! Come on, don't leave me hangin' here. Come on. No? All right.

"How about you, miss? No? Aww. Breaking my heart here....

"Winner every day, folks. *Every* day. Step right up... alright, here we go! Our next winner. What do you say, Vic, this one look like a winner to you?"

The vole vigorously shook his head side to side. "No? Now Vic, it's hard enough getting folks to step forward and give this a whirl. You're not exactly helping."

Vic leaned in for a whispered conference. "Well now, what's that you say, Vic? Getting volunteers is like pulling teeth?" Vic nodded his head *Yes*, deftly catching his head before it flew off and horrified the children in the front row. "It's funny you should say that, Vic. Young fella, come on up here and say a few words to the crowd....

"Don't wanna?

"Yeah, I kinda thought you might not. Damon, please, if you could...now hold *still*, friend, we don't want to hurt you…Damon, Johnny, hold him steady.…

"Ho-*lee* smokes, folks, can you all see that? Everybody see?" Johnny swiveled him around to face the crowd, and Damon twisted the young man's arm hard behind his back. "Haha…this is like roping a runaway calf, folks… hey, get Jules back here! Maybe he can give us a hand.…" Johnny reached up and held his chin so that he faced the crowd, then pinched the man's nostrils shut with his other hand. The man twisted and thrashed around, but Johnny and Damon held him tight. Vic Vole entertained the kids in the crowd by miming the man's struggling, then standing in front of him and hauling out an enormous pocket watch to time how long the man could hold his breath.

"Any second now…turning purple, friend, you'd better—ah, there we go. Good lungs there, buddy! Damon, hold his mouth open wide and show the crowd. Look at that, folks. Still a bloody mess in there. Anyone here know how much 32 teeth would weigh?"

"Well, *I* know.

"Folks, I've been doing this for a long time. A *long*, long time. Too many years.

"And not to blow my own horn too loudly, but there's not a trick in this racket that I ain't yet seen. Not that they don't still try! Heh…you use a local, kid? Novocaine? I'm guessing that's a *No*, otherwise your lips would still look puffy. And your gums look fine, no obvious disease, no white spots, blotchiness, which means he knocked out a mouthful of healthy teeth, folks. *Healthy teeth*. Yikes. Anything to steal a march on me, isn't that right, Vic?"

The vole nodded, more in sorrow than anger.

"Friend, you got to get up *real* early in the morning to put one over on me. Mighty early. Matter of fact, you might not want to go to sleep at all.

"Two-oh-five."

CLANG!

"Get on that scale.

"Now.

"Gentlemen, help our taciturn friend onto the scale. That's right. Pal, you keep struggling, you're liable to trip and fall, and my good friend Damon here might accidentally pull your arm out of its socket. Are you reading me?

"All right. Let's dance!"

Wah-wah-wah-waaaahhhh. "Two hundred and seven, *point* six. Sorry friend! Better luck next time! Might want to put some Anbesol on those gums, buddy. Gentlemen, if you please, escort our young friend around back, and please see to it he doesn't stumble and kick the shit out of himself. Thank you, boys.

"Who's next?

"Come on, now. No need to get discouraged. Right now's the ideal time to play, folks! I mean, it feels like we've used up six months' worth of bad luck just this afternoon. Step right up, don't be shy.

"All right, friend, come on up, then." *ooohWEEEooooh.* "Hold up. Hold it right there." Damon came over and wanded the man from head to toe; the wand began to squeal when it waved in front of the man's stomach. "Alright, friend. Lift your shirt, please…whoa! Hold on now! No, you won't be going anywhere, will he, David?" Another carny, standing in the back of the onlookers, made his way forward, snapping open the clasp on his holster as the crowd parted dutifully for him. "Johnny, help our guest with his shirt please. Folks! Folks, I'm gonna have to ask you to remain right where you are. I just couldn't have your day ruined with this unpleasantness, so we're gonna resolve the situation and get back to the game, and you guys are gonna have a grand old time here. And that's a personal promise.

"What's that, sir? Well, if you'd taken your shirt off like I asked, it wouldn't *be* ripped, now would it? Damon, go on." Damon wanded him again, and again got a squeal when the wand floated over the man's smooth, tanned stomach. "Well, sir. We've got something of a dilemma here, don't we."

"Please—"

"This here's a metal detector, friend. And that railing you walked past, that's a metal detector, too. And yet I don't see any metal! No metal belt buckle. No metal jewelry. No piercings. Any implants that might account for it? Of course not, because there're no surgery scars…see, folks? No scars.

"Well, now.

"Well, well, well.

"What's that, son? Speak up. Here, speak into this, just not too loudly."

"…p-please. Please, I, I…I'm sorry, I wasn't—"

"Oh, that's right. Heh. You weren't. But you are now, aren't you?"

"Yes, yes sir."

"Louder, son."

"*Yes, yes sir!*"

"Say, I like you, partner. What's your name?"

"Jeff, Jeff, I'm, I'm Jeff…"

"Well, Jeff. Here's the issue, as I see it, and you can correct me if I'm wrong. You're not *wearing* any metal. And you obviously haven't had any metal *put in* you, by way of the scalpel. And yet we're still getting…folks, please. Let's keep it quiet. David, if you'd…thank you.

"And yet we're getting a reading on you, Jeff.

"So that sorta narrows the possible scenarios down, doesn't it.

"We've got a couple options here. My good friends Johnny and Damon, here, can walk you out back. There's a little trailer there, see, with a chair in it, and a cabinet. And Johnny and Damon'll tie you down in that chair—"

"F-fuck, *fuck*, please, I didn't, please just let me *see* her, I'll do whatev—"

"And Damon'll open that cabinet, and inside there's a toolbox. Little rusted old toolbox. And inside that, he's got some special tools.

"He might use the butcher knife. Or, maybe the wire strippers.

"Or maybe, if he happens to have a long enough extension cord, he'll plug in the circular saw. See, the carpenters and the 'lectricians 'round here kinda come and go and take what they please from that shed—we're a very egalitarian lot, here, y'know—and there might not be a cord hanging up on the wall.

"And then again, there just might.

"So, why don't we…careful, son, careful…all right, give him room…here, son, just heave it up right into this bucket, here…wow! Folks, I wish you could see this. Jeff here's doing his best impression of a slot machine. That's it, one more, come on…hear that clanging, everybody? Will you look at that…"

He lifted the plastic bucket up and gave it a good shake. The contents sloshed and clanged as they splashed and slid back and forth. "Boy, some people just *need* to win, don't they. How much'd you say you swallowed, Jeff? A cupful of these arcade tokens? Maybe more?

"What's that, son, speak up…here you go. What's that you said?"

Jeff looked dazed. "You can't…you can't *do* this. You have to let us *go*."

"Oh, is that a fact? And what makes you say that, Jeff? Hell, this is the biggest crowd we've had all day. Any of you folks wanna leave?"

"*No*." That was the average of their reactions, there were a whole lot of spirited *Hell no*s and more than a few people who said nothing at all, whose silence said it all for them, but on the whole most of the responses were simply *No*. Listless, perfunctory, not all that sincere. Some of them stood stock-still, dead trees trying not to sway in the wind, willing themselves inconspicuous. He wanted to laugh at these saps; didn't they realize that made them stand out all the more?

There were over a dozen carnies watching now, some smiling and clapping, others standing watch with arms crossed. And two more mascots had shown up, as well— a blue-nosed furry primate and a humanoid with the face and fins of a giant fish—and unlike the peaceable Victor Vole, these two each held oversized, brightly-colored mallets by their sides.

"Murray Mandrill! Barry Cuda! What do you think those rascals are up to, huh, Vic? You boys want to step up and put your keisters on the line? Yeah, that's what I *thought*, heh heh heh...hey, scoot now, get away from there. Barry, you put that little boy down. Murray! Let go of that woman's breasts. Haha. You two don't behave yourselves, I'm gonna send Sheriff Vic down there to regulate. Isn't that right, Vic?"

Victor Vole nodded, pretending to roll up his sleeves and then smacking his fist into his palm. Murray and Barry made a show of scampering away from the crowd and cowering behind the wooden fence that kept the crowd penned in. Some of the little kids laughed at their antics, joined by several adults, whose barking laughter was a little too loud, a little too forced.

"All right, Jeff. Might as well get this over with."

"S-sir...sir, I, please, I don't have to...I'll go back to work, please, I'll *go back to work, I won't make trouble, just please—*"

"You won't make *trouble*, but will you make *change*? I was looking to play a few rounds of *Intergalactic Space Patrol*. Can I get five bucks worth of tokens?" Damon drove his fist into Jeff's back, sending him to his knees, and Johnny kicked him hard in the stomach. Jeff moaned and retched up another mouthful of bile and puke onto the wooden floor of the stage, along with a few more metal tokens. *Clink, clink, clink.* Damon pushed his face down into his own vomit with an elbow drop into the small of his back, which managed to pump out another mouthful of soupy fluid. "Aw, come on, Jeff, that's barely two bucks' worth. Dig deep, partner!" Johnny and Damon went to work on him, kicking and stomping. One boot to Jeff's face elicited a loud cracking sound, and he spat up blood and what was either a mangled coin or a broken tooth.

"All right, all right. We'll call that five, then. Come on, let's get him on his feet, boys…okay, considering we've relieved you of that heavy burden you were carrying… plus some stomach fluids, and then there's the teeth lying on the ground there…

"I am calling it…at…

"One *eighty*. One eighty exactly."

CLANG!

"Get him on the scale, fellas…who knows, Jeff, this might be your lucky day."

Jeff tried to struggle as the carnies lifted him to his feet, careful to pull him up by sections of his shirt that hadn't been slathered with bile and blood and that morning's breakfast. Jeff shook his head dizzily, hanging in their grasp, dead weight. Then Damon slipped a bit on the vomit-slick floor, not quite losing his balance but letting go of Jeff's shoulder for a few seconds.

That was all Jeff needed. "*No!*" He swung his fist out, catching Johnny right in the crotch. Johnny moaned and doubled over, and Jeff pinwheeled around over him, slipped, stumbled off the stage and caught himself, painfully, on outstretched hands. A disembodied murmur of panic bubbled up from the crowd. Jeff pushed himself up (heaving up a great sob of pain as he did so; from the way he held his right hand, he looked to have broken his wrist) and staggered through the crowd, shoving pant-suited grandmothers and obese schoolchildren to either side as other carnies tried to press their way towards him. Most of the crowd was paralyzed with shock at this deviation from the script...but a few, the ones who'd been here the longest, allowed themselves a vicarious thrill at Jeff's mad dash, doing their best to goad him on karmically. This sort of thing Did Not Happen and all of them wanted to be there the one day that It Did.

Oh, he might just make it. He was almost at the entrance to the booth. He might—

An enormous orange-and-purple mallet whistled as it swung across the entrance way, smashing into Jeff's sternum, and this time something *did* break. Jeff's feet left the ground comically, sliding up and out before him as he left the ground and sailed backwards. The kid behind the counter thought quickly and toggled the slide whistle sound effect. Jeff landed on his shoulder blades with a wet, smacking thud that knocked the wind out of him.

The crowd cleared away as Victor Vole somersaulted off the stage and ran to join the fun. Barry Cuda—it had been his hammer which had cut short Jeff's afternoon sprint—and Murray Mandrill stood on either side of Jeff, slamming their mallets down, and down, and down again. Victor joined them and stomped on Jeff's head with his big floppy purple sneakers. Some of the parents covered their children's eyes, or held their faces close to their own, telling them without words *Look at me, look at me, don't look at the bad man*; other parents just watched, stupefied, as the three mascots bludgeoned any trace of resistance or motion out of Jeff's body.

After a certain point it stopped being horrific, and just became repetitive and redundant. Like a cartoon. Jeff was no longer reacting to each hammer blow, but sometimes his limbs would flop around or twitch if they hit him just right.

"All right, all right, Vic, Murray, Barry…let's give the guy some air, you've had enough fun for now. Why don't you make room for our friends…that's it. Fellas, help Jeff there to his feet…." Three of the workers lifted Jeff up, one by the shoulders and two on either side of him, and hauled him slowly through the crowd towards the stage. His broken left arm flopped to one side at a peculiar angle, and a little girl in a pink-and-peach set of overalls reached out to touch his hand. Her father pulled her hand away and smacked it, chiding her to behave herself. By now the carnival workers had spread out in a loose oval around the stage, heavy flashlights and wrenches held at their sides.

"Jeff!

"Jeffy Jeff Jeffrey. Jeff, old son. Why'd do you make us do that?

"Nobody's above taking their turn here, are they? Isn't that right, folks? Any of you feel like you're too good to climb on up and be reckoned?"

"*No!*"

"So what makes you think you're special, Jeff? Hmm?

"Cat got your tongue?"

One of the carnies pulled Jeff's head up by his hair. One eye was hidden behind a swollen, purple mass of flesh; the other stared ahead without focus. Jeff's nose was mashed in flat, and his lower teeth had all been knocked out.

"Nothing to say, huh? Well all right, friend. Let's get this over with. One eighty. Friends, give him a hand." The guards lowered him onto the platform scale, tucking his legs beneath him and draping his limp form in a coil. A peninsula of shattered bone jutted through the meat of his left arm, embarrassingly obvious.

The kid behind the counter flicked the slide whistle.

And then, another sound, one not yet heard today: the Trumpets of Victory. *Dah-de-de-dah-DAH!!!* "Wait a minute! Wait a *minute*! Look at this right here, folks! One hundred and eighty-four pounds, and that's after having the almighty *shit* kicked out of him! How about that!

"Let's hear it for Jeff!"

The crowd clapped and cheered wildly, careful to not to lower their gaze towards the winner.

"Hey, I think I'm doing pretty well today. Pretty good track record. So I don't begrudge Jeff here his win." He reached down and dropped a plush yellow duck onto Jeff's unmoving body. "There you go, Jeff. You enjoy that toy, you earned it fair and square…

"You know, it just goes to show you, folks," he continued, as the guards hoisted Jeff up and lugged him over to the steps leading off stage, "there's a winner *every* day here.

"Winner every *hour*, practically.

"You wanna go next? All right, well step right up, ma'am. No rush, no rush, take your time. The day is young, and this fair's gonna stay open as long as it has to. As long as we *want* to."

He smiled.

"You know, ma'am…I hate to cast aspersions on your honor and all, but I couldn't help but notice you limping there.

"Would you be a sport and slip off that shoe, so we

can count those toes?"

The woman tried to summon up the nerve to resist, then slumped her head with a sigh and reached down to slide her shoe off.

It had been worth a shot.

GHOST LIGHTS

Scott T. Goudsward

Ben and Katie walked hand-in-hand down the crowded midway. On either side of the bustling road, game barkers yelled through megaphones and headset microphones. The air felt heavy with aromas of churros, fried dough, and pizza. Through the haze of people and curtains of stuffed animals hung from cargo nets, rides loomed in the distance and a barrage of lights and cacophony of music filled the air.

Ben leaned down and kissed Katie on the top of her head. Her blonde hair smelled like the citrus shampoo she used. She smiled and squeezed his hand. Ben returned the smile, then her brown eyes widened at the booth encroaching on their path.

"Buy me a corndog?" she asked.

"Really?"

"With mustard and if you're nice I'll let you kiss me later," she answered coyly.

"What if I want to kiss you now?" Ben's dark eyes sparkled with the lights of the midway.

"I never could resist you." She stood on tiptoes and kissed him deep on the lips.

"One corndog coming up," Ben said and started off. He yelled over the drone of the game barkers "You want a drink with that?" Katie stepped to the side to get out of the way of the rush of people. Spying a map of the park, Katie burrowed through the bodies on the road to read it. Her slim finger traced a path down the concourse and shrieked feeling a tap on her shoulder.

A corndog loomed, blurred in her vision, too close to focus. Ben held it with a grin across his face. She slapped his arm and took the treat.

"Did you get the...?"

He handed her two packs of mustard.

"You're the best."

They strolled past the games as she ate and the barkers tried to coerce their money from their pockets.

"We should quit school and work here," Ben exclaimed. "You can run the Tilt-A-Whirl and I'll sell kettle corn." He took a sip from a plastic cup and then offered it to Katie. "It's okay, its root beer."

"Diet?"

"Really?" Ben stopped a man with a pushcart going past and bought a bag of cotton candy. "I should have brought a toothbrush."

"We should have brought the dentist." Katie laughed, oblivious to the mustard at the corner of her mouth. Ben gently wiped it off with his thumb.

"Now what, Katie?" Ben spread his arms as if offering her the entire park. She nodded at a wall of stuffed animals-red puppies, yellow bears, giant blue giraffes, and a massive fuzzy unicorn.

"Do I need to say it?" Ben's shoulders slouched. He smiled and stuck out a hand. Katie took hold and was led from booth to booth trying to figure out the best and cheapest way to win her the unicorn. The fluffy nightmare might mean second base. Ben grinned and led her to the baseball toss.

A young man, laden with acne and a mop of brown hair all but leapt from the booth seeing them approach. In back of him were six bowling pins on a crate. Stuffed animals and other prizes hung from looped chords from the awning and inside the walls.

"What can I do you for, sir?"

"Sir? You're older than I am," Ben said. Katie squeezed his hand and giggled a little. "What's the story here? What do I do?" The barker pushed the rim of his cap up and grinned thinking he had gotten his next pigeon.

"It's easy as pie, sport. Can I call you sport?" Ben nodded at the attendant; he had a stained name badge pinned to his vest. *Hi, my name is Mark.* "All you need to do is knock those pins over, three throws for two bucks. Knock them over with one ball and you get your choice. Knock them over in two, I choose. If any pins still stand at the end, you lose."

"Which of the pins are glued down?" Katie asked. Mark put on his best *hurt* look and walked back to the crate. He swept his arms through the pins toppling them. Mark raised his eyebrows at Katie and reset the pins. The second and fifth pin had magnets in the bases. *No one uses glue anymore,* He thought.

Ben dug into his pockets and dropped a five and a single down on the counter. Mark reached into a basket and pulled out nine misshapen softballs. The bills disappeared into Mark's pocket before Ben could blink. He stepped to the side of the booth and looked Katie up and down while Ben took aim.

The first ball nudged the top of the pins, none fell.

The second ball took out four. While Mark reset the pins, Ben changed his stance and squeezed the ball. Mark stood and stepped to the side again, he ran the tip of his tongue over his lips looking at Katie, who was oblivious to his leering. Ben launched the ball side-armed, it hit the one-two pocket and the pins erupted.

Mark stood open mouthed as the last pin rolled off the crate. Katie jumped up and down and latched onto Ben for a hug. Ben smiled at Mark and ran his hands down Katie's back until his fingertips brushed her belt, he watched Mark's eyes follow his hands all the way down.

"One fluffy unicorn please," Katie said. Mark tugged on the cord and Katie caught it before he could touch it. Katie hugged the unicorn and kissed Ben on the cheek, he slid his arm around her waist and they walked deeper into the park.

They walked ride to ride, stealing small kisses where they could. When Katie liked a ride she led Ben over to it and the unicorn would stay planted firmly under the bar in her lap. She made the operator of the loop coaster hold the unicorn and swear nothing bad would happen to it. A quick bat of her eyes and Katie knew he was hers' to command. On the carousel, Ben rode his horse backwards so he could watch and talk to Katie.

"What's next?" Katie seemed lost in thought and then pointed to the end of the rides.

"Ferris wheel," she said and dragged him by the hand.

"I thought you didn't like heights?" Ben said.

"It might get a little cozy in the chair then." The look in her eyes was the same she gave to the roller coaster guy. He was doomed. Ben walked to the ticket booth and bought another pile of tickets for the last ride of the night;.Though he hoped this ride lead to a different kind of ride.

"I think you bought too many," Katie said.

"Then we'll just have to come back tomorrow." Ben smiled and leaned in for a kiss.

They stood in line, watching the wheel turn and the lights flash across the surface of the lake. High above, sky cars traveled the length of the park on cables. Finally it was their turn. Ben handed the operator a bundle of tickets, not counting them and not caring. Katie stepped into the cart, it swayed as she sat, and Ben followed her in. The operator closed the bar on their legs and pulled hard on it, rocking the cart more, but they were secure.

"We should have gotten a snack for the ride., Katie said.

"You've had ice cream, a corn dog, cotton candy, and somehow managed to eat my candy apple." Katie smiled and batted her eyes. "Yeah some kettle corn would rock about now."

The ride started slowly, they edged up a few feet at a time as each cart after them was loaded. Soon they were on the top, Katie leaned against Ben and he slipped his arm over her shoulder. They looked at the lights on the lake and smiled. The night sky was full of stars.

"Next time we come when there are fireworks. My brother knows the guy who runs the sky ride and we can sit high up and watch them."

"Next time?" Katie giggled and hugged the unicorn. The massive lighted wheel began to turn, music streamed out from hidden speakers. The lights on the wheel's spokes blinked in greens, reds and purples. The Ferris wheel continued on its course. Katie was lost in the lights of the park and Ben tried to lose his fingers under the collar of her shirt. She moved the unicorn to intercept his groping.

"I knew this would come in handy," she said.

"Why did I win that thing again?"

"I think you were planning something dastardly." She looked up and grinned. The Ferris wheel shuttered and stopped. Ben grabbed for the edges of the cart for support as Katie's hands shot out and grabbed the bar.

"What's happening?" She looked over the side of the cart. "Did you set this up?"

"No. I know the sky ride guy. This isn't me." They sat for a moment and waited.

"I'm getting cold." Ben slid an arm around her shoulder and rubbed her arm. She moved in closer for his body heat.

"There's no alarms, nothing. It's like they don't know we're up here," Ben said.

"It would be kind of romantic, up here, watching the sun rise across the lake. Romantic but cold."

Ben peered over the side of the cart, it rocked with his movement. Out in the park, near the entrance a section of lights blinked out.

"See that," he said pointing. "They're having electrical problems." Katie patted down her pockets and dug through her small purse.

"I left my phone in your car."

"I think I forgot mine in your bedroom."

"We're doomed," she said and slid down in the cart. The piped in music crackled and stopped. Ben looked over the side again, the operators booth was empty, the inside light dark. The door hung open and batted against the side with each passing breeze. Ben hissed as another block of lights blinked out.

"Hey, down there," he yelled. "Can you hear me?" He leaned further over the side, holding tight to the bar. "Anyone?" The car below them was empty and the one below that. Ben spun, his legs mashed against Katie's. The carts across the wheel were also devoid of passengers.

"What do we do?" Katie screamed on the verge of hysteria. The midway went dark; the overpowering music funneled in through pole mounted speakers went dead.

"How loud can you scream, Katie?"

They took turns screaming as the park's perimeter went dark. With the strange quiet, the creak and squeal of the rocking cart became more pronounced. The colored lights on the spokes of the wheel went out one by one, like invisible hands turning them off. Katie stopped yelling when her throat was raw, her eyes watered with each dry swallow. Ben handed her the root beer cup with little more than a sip of melted ice left. A trickle of fear raced down his spine as he shivered more from fear than cold.

Then as if a superior power snapped its fingers, the rest of the park went dark. No rides, no booths, no games. Rides that had been in motion moments earlier stopped dead in their tracks. Ben glanced across the park at the skeletal frame of the wooden coaster. A train of cars stopped halfway up the first hill. No one there waved, or screamed. Something dropped them into a nightmare. Katie went to scream and stopped mid inhale. She huddled closer to Ben.

"What do we do?"

"Wait it out, see what happens." Ben kissed the top of her head, a weak attempt at comforting. She placed her head on his chest. "Go ahead and sleep, I'm not going anywhere."

"You better not," she whispered. Ben looked out over the lake. On the far side was a small sand beach he had taken other girls for "dates." There was a small dock for kayaks and swimming, it was used more for sex and keeping beer coolers out of the water. You could swim in the lake, near the shore but not fish. The fireworks barge and debris that fell every Wednesday and Saturday April through September, kept the water undrinkable and barely safe enough to swim in. A smile played across his lips thinking back to his last time on the beach.

Ben continued his lookout using the moon for its light, not feeling safe under its watchful gaze. As the night cooled, fog rolled in across the lake. By midnight the park was in a shroud of white. Katie started awake rubbing her eyes.

"Is it cloudy?"

"It's fog," Ben said. He pulled his sweatshirt off and draped it over Katie.

"You'll freeze."

"I'm not cold," he said, smiling.

"You look so worried." She sat up rocking the cart back and forth on the supports. One of the lights shook loose and fell to an explosive death in the fog below.

"Stop shaking us," Ben barked.

"Sorry." She whispered.

The speakers in the cart hissed and crackled, this time Ben rocked the cart violently trying to spin around.

"Someone is here," he said. He looked out over the park. The moon gave a slight illumination to the thick fog. No car lights, no flashlights.

"Did you see someone?"

Ben shook his head. Katie screamed and pointed over the side. The stuffed unicorn slid off her lap and dropped into the car below them. She grabbed for it, but the lap bar held her in place.

"Down there," she said.

Figures moved through the fog, colored hazes that moved as they watched. Ben yelled and shouted; waved his sweatshirt like a flag and not one of them responded.

As he watched, two of the figures moved through each other. He sat back hard against the metal back of the chair.

"We're dreaming," he whispered. "We have to be." Katie took his hand in hers and kissed his fingertips. Ben slid down in the chair a little, feeling defeated his plans for the evening eradicated before coming close to fruition. The wheel jerked and turned a few inches. Katie screamed at the sudden motion. Big Band music crackled and then streamed out from the speakers. The brass of trumpets, trombones and an easy jazz beat filled the park.

Katie screamed again when the wheel turned. They rotated slowly, Ben tried to figure out when they'd be close to the ground.

"I'm going to jump and go for help."

"You are so not leaving me here!"

The wheel jerked to a stop.

"We're still high up. If we move again, you have to be ready to jump." Ben grabbed the bar and strained at it, trying to get enough space to get their legs free. Katie latched on to his arms. Ben felt her fingernails digging into the flesh on his arm. She was pale and her eyes bulged. He looked to see what she was staring at. There were people in the car below them. Young lovers, hand in hand stealing a kiss in the moonlight.

"Hey! Up here!" Ben yelled. They paid him no heed, like he was invisible. When Ben went for a better look, he saw they were translucent. "I can't wait to wake up!" Ben twisted around, trying not to mash or mangle Katie against the cart, the other carts were full and he had the strange sensation of moving, but the wheel was still. The main thoroughfare was luminescent with the moving figures, like fireflies in the mists.

"They're talking," Katie said. "I can't hear them." Katie

watched their lips move trying to read the words; they were at too odd an angle. The ghost couple stopped for a moment and looked up at her. Their eyes were solid white, lips cold and pale. The woman smiled politely and waved a little wave. "Oh my God," Katie whispered and pinched Ben.

The couple was aging. The man was dressed in an old army uniform. His hair grayed and slid from scalp. Lines and wrinkles appeared and cracked around her eyes and mouth. Soon teeth were dropping like ghost stones into the fog below. Their arms became thinner, skin dried and changed from healthy pink to a spotted yellow. Their shoes dropped off, socks hung limp on curling toes, bones from their feet poking through the desiccated cloth. The woman collapsed against the soldier and then he slumped against the side of the cart and toppled over the wall. Down below in the fog, the lights were going out, the colored shapes faded and fell.

Ben twisted around again, this time pulling his legs out from under the bar. He knelt in the cart and peered over the back wall. The same was happening in the other carts. Couples aged and died slipping out of the ride and into the fog.

Katie started crying.

"What is it?" He asked. Ben lifted her face and wiped away a tear with his thumb. A streak of gray colored her hair and the skin on her hand was spotted.

"What's happening to me?" Ben cried out as his knuckles bent, twisted and swelled. Agony washed over him as arthritis took hold. He went to look at Katie, his eyes suddenly clouded and hazed. He stared at his bent hand and gnarled fingers. Katie cried into her hands. Her gray hair thinned, the scalp below visible. Her back was now hunched and bowed.

"Every time one of them disappears, we get older," he wheezed. He looked over the side of the cart as the last of the figures faded from sight. Katie's crying stopped and a cracked wheeze escaped her lips. A tear slipped down Ben's wrinkled cheek as the last breath escaped.

The fog grew thicker and the booths vanished until the last thing in existence in the park was the old Ferris wheel. Ben's arm hung limp from the cart as dawn broke over the lake. When the fog was dissolved by the sun's warmth, the park was gone. No tents, booths or stands. The only thing left on the weed-choked grounds, was the skeletal remains of the old Ferris Wheel.

ABRAHAM'S ABOMINATIONS

PAMELA M. NIHISER

"The carnival is in town!" Luke yelled with excitement.

"What carnival?" his mother asked. "I haven't heard of any carnival in town for years."

"It's in the field just outside of town, Mom," Luke said, irritated.

His mother stood over the sink finishing the last of the dishes. "Well, maybe I missed the advertisements somehow." She rolled her eyes. " But it doesn't matter anyway, Luke, you know you can't go. You're still grounded from when you and Joseph toilet papered Mister Jones' tree and threw his cat into the river. Don't you remember that? "

"Yes. But, Mom, Joseph is coming over right now! His mom is letting him go. Besides, that was a week ago. I've been good. Plllllleeeeeaaassseee!"

Luke knew if he played his cards just right his mom would always give in to him. All he had to do was make those big puppy eyes at her. And that is exactly what he did.

"OK! Just clean your room first. Then you can go."

"Yes!"

Luke hurried up the stairs to his room. He stood at his bedroom door for a moment, contemplating his course of action. Luke finally decided that shoving everything in his closet was his best bet. He shoveled it all in with his hands and slammed himself up against the door to make sure it shut all the way. Socks and pants hung out the sides but he didn't care. As far as he was concerned his job was done.

There was a knock at the door.

"Joseph!" Luke yelled as he sprinted down the stairs.

His mother stopped him before he could reach the door. "Did you get your room cleaned, Luke?" she asked with her arms folded.

"Yes, Mom! Can I go now? Can I go now? Can I go now?"

"Well...." She paused and looked down at the floor. "I suppose so. But, be careful. There can be some shady people at those carnivals. A lot of children go missing around those places. Don't you go runnin' off with the carnies. "

"Oh you're just being paranoid. Thanks, Mom!" Luke barked as he hurriedly grabbed his jacket and ran out the door.

Luke stepped outside to see his long time friend and partner in crime, Joseph, patiently waiting on him. Joseph's long blond hair covered his face as he stared down at the ground. He impatiently kicked at the rocks lining the driveway. As he saw Luke approach, he picked up a small pebble and smacked him in the head with it.

"Ow!" Luke yelled.

"That's for taking so long." Joseph said.

"I had to pick up my room."

"You just shoved everything in the closet then?" Joseph smirked.

"Hell yeah I did!"

"Lets get out of here before she finds out., Joseph said as they took off down the dirt road.

"Did your mom give you any money?" Luke asked.

"No, she never does. I did take a five dollar bill out of her wallet though. But that's all I could find. She probably won't even notice it's gone until later anyway. I'm pretty sure she won't care. She never does."

Luke stopped in his tracks. He always looked up to Joseph. He was a trouble maker but he was the coolest guy Luke knew. It was if he had no fear. He did whatever he wanted when he wanted to. And, to him, it was fascinating how he always got away with it. His mother never punished him anymore. She used to, but Joseph was in trouble so much that she pretty much just gave up. As a matter of fact, he had the house to himself most of the time. Lucky him. Luke's mother was always in his business and it drove him insane. She'd cry all the time when he got in trouble. But Luke didn't care. He wanted to be cool like Joseph.

"Wow! You're so lucky, Joseph. Your mom lets you do whatever you want. I wish mine was like that."

"Yeah. I like it. You need to get her more irritated. Eventually she'll leave you alone."

"Yuck. My mom is way too bossy. She grounds me every time I get in trouble. I just got off grounding from when we toilet papered Mister Jones' house and killed his cat. Sheesh!" he scratched his head. "No one has a sense of humor anymore."

Joseph giggled. "We just need to be a little more stealthy next time. Look! We're here!"

Luke and Joseph came to the crest of the hill. They stood staring at the amount of tents that rose to the skyline. There were so many. Excitement took over the both of them. They raced down the hill while music filled their ears and the smell of sugary treats filled their nostrils.

They approached the ticket booth. A tall, very slender man, who resembled a skeleton, leaned over the table and glared a them.

"Welcome to the carnival! That will be two dollars and fifty cents each please." He unrolled his long fingers out towards them.

"That's all you have," Luke mumbled to Joseph.

"Don't worry about it. We're crafty. We just need to get in, right?"

Joseph pulled out the five dollar bill and placed it in the man's boney hand.

"Thank you," he said while displaying a crooked tooth grin. "Enjoy yourselves, boys!"

Luke and Joseph wandered around the grounds, debating on what they wanted to do first.

"Let's get some cotton candy." Joseph smiled, sheepishly.

"Dude, we're broke."

"I told you. Don't worry about it."

Joseph made his way to the cotton candy booth. He waited patiently for the carny to turn his back. He then, swiftly, grabbed two cotton candies and bolted. The carny was none the wiser.

"See?" Joseph smiled. "No worries!"

Luke frowned, but he went along with it, then laughed. "Perhaps you should join the carnival. You could be Ninja Man or something like that."

"Boy, that name is lame, But being a carny would be mega cool." Joseph paused in front of a large tent and stared up. "Oh, we are going in here!"

Luke stopped to see what had grabbed Joseph's attention. The sign above the tent opening read "Abraham's

Abominations."

"Abominations?" Luke asked. "Like a freak show?'

"Yes it is. Let's go."

"No." Luke stepped back. "It costs money anyway."

Joseph began to taunt him. "Oh! Someone is scared. Pussy!"

"I am not!" Luke yelled and straightened his back."I just think there are more fun things to do besides that."

"Suit yourself, ya pansy! I'm going in!"

"I am not a pansy!" Luke yelled.

Luke's outburst caught the attention of a man sitting just inside the tent.

"Can I help you boys?" he asked as he stood up, revealing how tall he was. His clothes hung on him loosely and the raggedy top hat he wore was pulled so far down on his forehead that his eyes were barely visible.

"No," Luke replied. "We're just looking."

"Really?" The man said as he exhibited a rotten toothed smile. "Are you afraid? Do you have a problem with freaks, boy?"

"No, sir," Luke conveyed. "It just costs money and we don't have any right now."

"Well, that's all you had to say, son. We can do what's called an Annie Oakley."

"Annie Oakley? What is that?" Joseph asked as he stood next to Luke.

"It's when I give you two free passes. You boys seem worthy to me. What do ya say?"

"Absolutely!" Joseph grinned. "Thank you, sir."

"Call me Abraham."

Joseph ran through the opening in the tent. He left Luke standing there, alone, with the strange man.

"Oh! You are afraid." The carny smirked as he poked Luke in the chest.

"I'll show you!" Luke exclaimed as he marched

through the door.

The man leaned his head through the opening. "Enjoy the show, boys. Nice to have ya aboard."

Luke stopped. "What does he mean by that?"

"Who knows and who cares? Now shut up and lets go look!"

Joseph and Luke made their way through the hallway entrance to a large opening in the middle of the tent. Around the outskirts of the tent were iron cells, each one lit by a single dim light bulb hanging from a rope from the roof. In front of each squared off area was a sign describing who you were looking at. It reminded Luke of a zoo.

The first cell they approached was a little girl with facial hair. A long mustache and beard covered the lower half of her face. She said nothing. Just stared at the boys as they walked by. There was sadness in her eyes.

The second display was a large jar sitting on a table. It contained what appeared to be a half monkey half fish specimen.

Joseph read the sign out loud. "Mermaid." He rolled his eyes. "Whatever."

"Eh, this isn't so bad." Luke said. "I don't see what the big deal is."

The third spectacle was of two young girls that sat beside each other on a sofa. He could barely see them in the dim lighting. They only thing that seemed odd to Luke about them is they were both missing their arms.

"Siamese twins," Joseph read from the sign. As he looked up, the two girls stood up and began to limp towards them. They were connected at the waist. They're bodies clunked together as they made their way forward. The girl on the right tripped, taking the other one down with her. They lay face down, crying.

"Weirdos," Joseph scoffed and walked off.

"Where are you going? They need help," Luke said as he made his way under the ropes.

"Screw that! This is dumb! I'm out of here. It wasn't even worth the free admittance. I don't even want to see the rest of it!" Joseph ran out the back door, again leaving Luke alone.

"I'm sorry! My friend is a jerk," Luke said as he squatted down next to the girls. "Let me help you up."

He carefully rolled the two girls over. What he saw terrified him. Both of their mouths had been sewn shut.

"Shit!" Luke yelled as he stumbled back in terror.

One of the girls lifted what was left of her arm towards Luke in a plea for help. This was not some medical deformity they had. Their arms were removed. The ragged stumps had not even completely healed. Blood oozed from the torso of their dress as the girls tugged against each other trying to free themselves.

Luke backed up and stared around the tent. All of the freaks were children. They clamored towards the end of their cells letting out muffled cries. There were children with extra limbs that hung lifeless, some without any at all, children that were joined to others, children that resembled frogs, alligators and other reptiles. All of them had their mouths sewn shut.

I've got to call the police.

Before he could turn around he was struck on the head and everything went black.

"Help! Help! Get me the hell out of here!"

Luke awoke to hear Joseph screaming. His head was still foggy and his eyesight had not yet adjusted. Everything was blurry. He saw what appeared to be a bright light hanging right over him. He felt cold steel beneath him. He then realized he was laying on a table.

"Uh." He moaned. "What is going on?"

"Welcome to the carny family, boy! Are you scared? You should be."

Luke's eyes focused just in time to see the creepy man from outside the tent staring down at him. He noticed a stabbing pain in the lower half of his body that made him want to assume the fetal position, but he was unable to. Something was wrong with his legs. As a matter of fact, he couldn't even feel his legs at all.

"What the hell?"

He kept hearing Joseph screams. "Oh my God! Let me go! I won't tell anyone! Please!"

Luke reached his hand down and felt the stitches. He raised himself onto his elbows and looked down. In the place of his legs was Joseph. They had been sewn together at the abdomen. Luke glanced over at the corner of the room and saw both his and Joseph's lower halves just tossed in the corner.

He began to scream.

"Oh, shut your mouth! You can slink on the ground like the little snakes you are," the carny said. "Now you'll always be able to hang out. Isn't this what you wanted? Oh and I did a little facial reconstruction too. Opinion?"

He held up a mirror and angled it just right. To Luke's horror, his face was covered in hair and his nose had been sawed down, his upper lip had been cut in an upside down V and he had whiskers. Both of his ears had been cut to resemble a feline's. His eyes widened.

"Hmmm. Poor cat, huh? You little bastards," the man grumbled.

"Why? Why did you do this to us?"

"You see, this carnival shows up where the bad apples are. We have kids from all over the world. And you both drew us here. You caused your family strife. We're your family now!"

The man made his way over to a table in the corner of the dingy room. Blood was splattered all over the inner walls. He picked up some string and a hooked needle off of a small surgical table and stood over Joseph. Luke watched as he stuck the needle through Joseph's lips and pulled the thread through. Joseph screamed in agony. Luke watched Joseph cringe with each insertion. The man repeated the action until his mouth was completely sewn shut.

"Now, your turn, you little shit! You're going to be a nice addition. You'll bring in the dough. Maybe I'll throw you a few cat treats here and there. Now hold still."

Luke screamed as the needle was inserted into the corner of his mouth. He tried to turn his head to avoid another stab from the needle but the man wrapped his long fingers around his forehead and held him firmly in position.

Abraham smiled down at him. "I bet you regret everything you've done now, don't you? Bet you wish you could take it all back? Too late. Welcome to hell!"

As he began to black out he heard Abraham scream, "Come one! Come all! See Abraham's new abomination, The cat-faced conjoined twins!"

CALLIOPE

GREGORY L. NORRIS

He wanted to kill her. Just walk right up when nobody was looking, aim his foot at her face, drive it into her smile—her goddamn fucking *smirk*—and smile back as his size twelve blasted through her expression. The satisfaction might last. More than likely, Hugo suspected it wouldn't, a temporary fix to a far bigger problem.

The grains of her flesh would cling to the hair on his legs, stick between his toes, but Hugo would get away with killing the woman on the beach. Hustle down to the water, wash her off his epidermis, all evidence vanishing into the Atlantic. Hypothetical homicide wasn't the problem; the kicker was, Hugo didn't know if he'd be able to stop from pressing deeper once the waves knocked him off his feet. It dawned-while he sucked the cancer stick down to the filter and calliope music pulsed and clanked across the beach and smiling people built sand sculptures, and sand women—that drowning in the swells off Hollings Head, Rhode Island might be a better option than this cursed existence.

The image of his cross trainers, tattered and sweaty on the sand beside his bare feet, stoked Hugo's rage. He bought the sneakers less than a month before, but working the merry-go-round had ruined them. Nothing here retained its newness, especially people. Hugo was twenty-three going on seventy. Hell, the bikini-clad piece of ass being crafted on the beach some dozen yards away was comprised of grains pounded by a billion years worth of tides. Hatred for the bitch bloomed, though they had only just met over the course of his lunch break. Hugo choked down the last of the corn chips in a bag too small to satisfy his hunger, chugged a soda made warm and flat in the afternoon sun, and pondered committing the crime. Not much of one in a world going steadily unhappier and crazier with each season; the victim, not even a real woman.

The salt air burned in his lungs. The meager lunch, all he could afford, clawed at the soft lining of Hugo's gut. Oblivious artists crafted castles, a sphinx, sun and moon faces, a pirate ship, and one smirking bikini babe as part of the zillionth annual sand sculpture contest. She looked washed ashore, horny and in need of a devastating kick to the head.

Oh, the temptation.

He'd make the local evening news, maybe the national. Go viral. Get his own reality TV show. Be reviled universally when his brief time in the spotlight waned, like those women with all the bastard babies or the dude with multiple wives. Hugo Glennly, murderer of make-believe beach bunnies. He'd surely get canned from working the rides, be forced out of his rented room in a house where everything stunk of the ocean and the air was too thick to breathe.

Instead, Hugo tossed the wrapper and the dregs of his soda bottle in a garbage barrel buzzing with grateful flies, grabbed his sneakers, and about-faced. He shot a scowl over his shoulder and made the connection as to why he wanted to cave in the woman's skull. To not only destroy her face but also ruin the day for her sculptor and everyone else flocking to watch her ascension from the sand.

She reminded him of the faces of the Four Winds carved onto the ceiling of the carousel. One of those winds had blown Hugo to the seaside community; the gusts had stalled, and now he was stuck.

Just walk into the waves and end it, urged a voice in his thoughts. Before you really do kill someone. A body made of blood and bone, not sand.

Hugo ignored the dialogue, lit another cigarette, and navigated through the tight press of bodies and the swampland of human smells along the boardwalk, the dirge of calliope music growing steadily louder on his return march to the merry-go-round.

The loud and clanking contraption first inspired the young to squeal—and many, no doubt, to scream in terror—sometime in the 1950s, according to a sign spelling out its storied history. It had traveled from the coast of Maine all the way to Hollings Head at the end of the previous spring, bought at a bankruptcy auction from another amusement park. Hugo took a shorter route, not even twenty miles south from Bristol. But over the summer months, the walk assumed the ominous qualities of that fabled thousand in the Japanese proverb. Or was it Chinese? Hugo couldn't remember.

Hugo feared boundaries were being blurred and that he was starting to imagine things as a direct result of running the ancient collection of gears and grease, and the multitudes of vacant eyes captured in an instant of fright—horses with mouths frozen open in silent screams and showing plenty of teeth, their saddles and reins studded with fat, fake jewels—staring at him, always staring. Among the carousel horses were other fantastical creatures: walruses and undersea mer-people, male and female, the latter with scallop shells or starfish for bra cups over scandalously large tits. Hugo sometimes wondered how many confused young men would rub out their first orgasms to thoughts of the she-kelpies spinning round and round beneath their sweating flesh after they staggered down the exit ramp, their dirty dreams set to the pounding calliope soundtrack. More than once, after checking to make sure that nobody but the horses were watching, he, too, had felt up the scallop shells and thrown wood in his cargo shorts as a result.

The domed roof above the merry-go-round bore an intricate galaxy of painted stars and planets, along with carved faces representing the Four Winds. All were depicted as female.

A quartet of cold bitches, Hugo thought, unable to look at them as he approached the control booth.

The merry-go-round sat inert. The line of waiting riders stretched from the Minimum Height Chart halfway to the pizza shack directly next door. Calliope music pulsed regardless, a constant, drumming tribal beat that had imprinted on Hugo's gray matter. After eight hours of manning the controls, he often woke in the night with a brutal headache, the music ricocheting off the insides of his skull. Lights flashing off carousel mirrors scattered his dreams apart and added to his growing inability to separate what was real from that which wasn't.

A dusty smell hung about the contraption, like a room in a forgotten part of a big house sitting bottled up with the doors closed, baking whenever the sun shone through a gap in the curtains. The pizza place sold what tasted like cardboard with sauce and cheese tossed over it. When the ocean breeze fell flat, the combination of aged wood and thin-crust was nauseating.

No wind blew, and the merry-go-round exuded its fetor of stagnant places mixed with bad beach pizza.

"You're late," snapped Monroe.

"I got lost in the crowd," Hugo lied, not meeting the older man's eyes.

Monroe huffed an expletive beneath his breath. "Don't be surprised if I take an extra twenty, too, out there in the population explosion."

He slapped the keys onto Hugo's palm hard enough to sting. The hurt brought Hugo out of the fog, but not his misery. Without painting on a smile, he took to the microphone.

"Step on up, folks, for the happiest ride in Hollings Head…"

Scowling, he took their tickets.

The sun sank behind the arcades, a bloated red giant. A moon equally vast, distorted by the atmosphere, slowly jacked itself up from the ocean. One of the Four Winds blew a cooling breath, making the humidity bearable.

The music clanked, crescendoed, and continued without interruption. The carousel circled around and around, driven into motion by the push of the big green button, until Hugo stabbed the red switch that slowed the terrified ponies and mer-folk and walruses, driving them into reverse.

At a point just after dusk, the joyous shrieks of a child from somewhere in that cycloning illusion warped time and space, and briefly Hugo remembered what it was like to be happy.

Monroe snapped at him to wake up, and Hugo's visit to the past ended. He was back in Hollings Head, serving time and suffering the aches of a man twice his age. Worse, the absence growing inside seemed to say that he was already planted in the crypt, one more unfortunate doomed to wander Limbo, land of lost souls.

Smoking helped.

It didn't really, but Hugo sold himself on the idea that without coffin nails, without *something* to distract him from the shitty summer job and the endless clanking dirge pumped out of speakers from nine in the morning until eleven at night, he'd start facing his reflection in the mirror and see—truly *see*—the image gazing back and all of the failure it embodied.

He was never going to college. He'd never own a new car or a house. Anyone he fucked would be of a certain class, *class-less*, low-shelf. Life was never going to get any better. Add the likelihood of emphysema and lung cancer into the mix, and the urge to walk away from the merry-go-round, head down to the beach, to walk into the water and keep on walking, ruined sneakers and all, very nearly overwhelmed him.

This wasn't the life he'd dreamed for himself.

And it didn't help that Hugo had started to see things.

On the way home, he stopped at the corner store and bought a cheap bottle of scotch. If the lungs didn't do him in, the liver was a decent enough backup plan.

High tide pounded the beach in counterpoint to the calliope music still cycling through his skull, the waves heard but not seen from the dark front stoop where Hugo nursed a building buzz. His head would be in pieces by the morning. Just after midnight, he considered taking that very long swim beneath the full moon but was too tired to make the effort at ending his life.

The lease to the first floor apartment in the beaten-up old New Englander was in Aubrey James Paris's name, which meant there wasn't much Hugo could do about the mess in the kitchen other than clean it up himself. Dishes sat stacked in the sink higher than when he'd left that morning, and a sour smell hung about the place. Aubrey had claimed the big bedroom; no argument there. But one or more of his guests for the night had also monopolized the shower, according to the laughter filtering through the closed door to the apartment's only bathroom. The shower ran, worsening Hugo's misery. He considered relieving himself in the sink but instead watered the scrubby juniper trees in what passed for the house's front yard.

Dirty laundry formed two growing piles beside his bed. Before passing out, sweaty and with his stomach curdling worse by the moment, Hugo wondered if he had anything clean to wear to work in the morning. Then he remembered that he didn't care whether he woke up or not, and sank into a deep sleep haunted by the clanks and bells of the carousel, glowing among the splintered golden flashes in his dreams and nightmares.

He woke in the bald light of another muggy July

morning, soaked with tainted sweat. Hugo's body had leached an oily outline into the top sheet, and a foul taste lay thick atop his tongue. The day broke no different from the ones before it. No wonder his soul had been annihilated.

Hugo sat on the stoop in his shorts and smoked. Maybe he should get a cat, he thought. A humorless chuckle worked around the filter. A cat would give him something to care about, other than cigarettes. Then he remembered the no pets clause in Aubrey's lease. And why should he condemn any creature, even a cat, to sharing in his misery? The only other prick who deserved this life was Aubrey.

The screen door croaked open.

"Hey," Aubrey said.

"Hey," Hugo answered.

Their conversations had degenerated to basic greetings in recent weeks after Hugo's second time late with his half of the rent. Aubrey smelled showered. Whatever lay or lays from the previous night had screwed and scooted. Aubrey walked past the junipers and out of sight, no doubt headed for work.

How easy it would be to wander back inside, drop his lit cigarette somewhere flammable in that sty, and walk away, too. To let it burn. Burn it to the ground. Walk into the ocean and wait for the calliope music to mercifully fade.

Thunderheads charged in during the late morning, dropping a warm shower that clung unpleasantly to the skin. The rain didn't cool the humidity but worsened it; it did, however, thin the crowds.

Hugo saw her for the first time while he pondered for the dozenth or hundredth the series of unfortunate choices that had led him to this time and place. She moved through the pedestrian traffic with relative ease, more wind than flesh. She would have stood out on any day, stormy or sun-lit, but on this afternoon her mane of hair trailing behind her, a red too fiery to be natural, a color closer to that of fresh blood, radiated with wild and unapologetic majesty. A short-sleeved top, red as well, over a voluminous denim skirt, the view from the back lent an illusion of youth; some unbridled young woman who smelled of roses, her fragrance narcotic, her confident stride unleashing unfamiliar emotions through Hugo's core.

When he saw her the second time, in line to ride the merry-go-round, the question of the woman's age was answered in the wrinkles around eyes and mouth, blemished skin in folds at the neck, and a cross note from the pizza shack that transformed her floral scent into something funereal.

What startled Hugo most were her eyes. Sun-washed blue, like the color of the ocean in the tropics, they reflected the light from the carousel mirrors, almost not there. While taking tickets, he tracked their ghostly gaze to the merry-go-round. What he saw in her study was a suggestion that the rest of the world no longer existed. There was only the antique wooden horses, the painted galaxy overhead, mirrors and moonbeams.

She handed him her ticket.

"One?" Hugo asked.

The woman blinked. He appeared without warning into the canvas of her small world as the pale mirrors of her eyes trained on him. "One, yes," she said.

She smiled. He existed. As the woman sauntered past, he noticed her hips were significantly wider in their co-

coon of denim. She wasn't even pretty in the accepted sense of the world, but to Hugo she suddenly became the most beautiful creature in all the cosmos. He was an extension of the carousel. He *was*.

"Enjoy the ride," he said.

"Oh, I will. I've been waiting for this for a very long time."

The woman brushed past, her scent of roses returned to its magnificence up close. Hugo drew in a deep breath. For a wonderful moment, he was young again, splashing in puddles while rain fell and golden sunlight spilled down from the sky.

The sun shower from that other life quickly shorted out.

"This century," some sour-faced mother of two snapped, pushing him again toward the edge of the water.

He took their tickets and started the ride.

The calliope music pulsed and jangled. The guts of the original steam-driven apparatus had been yanked out and replaced by electronics well before the merry-go-round's arrival to Hollings Head, but as the carousel began its revolutions, picking up speed, the melody built, became the heartbeat of a waking, ancient dragon in Hugo's imagination.

The horses ran in circles. While children shrieked mostly in joyous voices, Hugo tracked the woman, that beautiful creature, to a white carousel horse with pink and sapphire jewels studded in its bridle and saddle. Between blinks and revolutions, the red-haired woman gyrated. The way she gripped the reins and rode the pommel, her denim skirt billowing behind her, head tossed back, drew a portrait of a woman at her most aroused.

The elegance, the *audacity*, caused Hugo's manhood to vibrate in concert with the music. His breaths came with increasing difficulty. The merry-go-round spun, and

Hugo envisioned the woman grinding her hips, clenching and unclenching her sex around the pommel, one hand caressing the horse's carved mane while the other clutched at the reins for balance.

Humping the pommel, riding the calliope horse for unimagined destinations, she looked younger, wilder; hot and happy. Perhaps the last trace of true happiness left in the entire universe. A smile broke on Hugo's face. He fought it, failed. She rode the horse with the pink and sapphire gemstones, and Hugo let the merry-go-round cycle, around and around, forward and backwards, twice the normal time allotted.

He studied her, aware of his erection pinned at an awkward angle between leg and underwear leg band. The way she eased off the calliope horse, choreographed to the music and strobing splinters of reflected light, worsened Hugo's discomfort: liquid and elegant, she slipped down, smoothing the folds of her denim skirt, an understated grin on her lips.

Forcing his legs into motion, Hugo hurried out of the control booth, wincing with the steps. But she was gone between the golden flashes, and those waiting in line made their growing hostility known in tisks and clearer messages.

"You'd fuckin' better give my kids the same amount of time, dude," said an angry man in an orange wife-beater whose arms were covered in ink.

"Yeah, sure," Hugo said, less from fear, more to stem the anger already starting to feast on the tiny spark of goodness returned to his world. "But first, I need to check—"

He didn't finish the sentence. No one was listening, anyway. Hugo jumped up the well-traveled metal steps and onto the merry-go-round, shuffled between horses and sea kelpies, his cock complaining, his heart in a gallop. The white horse with the jeweled saddle drew closer, its white eyes tracking his progress. In the glittering lights, he swore the antique wooden animal smiled, too, the terror gone from its expression.

The pommel glistened with fresh wetness in the lights. Hugo didn't realize he had stopped breathing until the last bottled sip began to burn in his lungs. His next hit of air smelled sweet and magical, perfumed with roses and honey.

Rain hammered Hollings Head.

Hugo walked back to the apartment in no hurry, splashing through puddles. His socks squished in his wet sneakers. He didn't care. He was close to happy.

Reaching into his pants, he fondled his thickness without guilt or worry. The rain cleansed the night, washing away the stagnant saline of the ocean and replacing it with the scent of flowers. His last cigarette had been smoked hours earlier; the thought of another held no interest. Hugo didn't need a smoke; all he wanted was the red-haired woman.

He opened the bedroom windows and stripped in the dark to the music of the rain. On any other night in Hollings Head, the melody would have depressed him, no better than the pulsing dirge of the carousel. Now, he felt rejuvenated, baptized. Peeling off his wet clothes aided in the rebirth. Naked, he felt lighter in both body and spirit. The breeze rose. Raindrops scattered. Fresh air whispered over his flesh. Hugo was tempted to turn on the lights, but doing so would cast a harsh note of reality and reestablish the truth of his surroundings. But in the dark, the illusion that his world had somehow been transformed by a divine visitation persisted.

She had given him back his life.

Hugo stretched across the bed, tipped his face toward the nearest window, and drew in a deep breath. He masturbated twice and then curled into a fetal pose. Sleep claimed him almost instantly.

Hugo woke to the notes the rain struck on the windowsill. He sat up. The sad rented room materialized through a moody filter of gray, and the smile on his lips surrendered.

He knew he had to find her. The red-haired woman was his last chance at happiness.

What could he offer her in return? Not much in the way of a life, he knew, again aware of the invisible weight pressing down upon his shoulders. Hugo had seventy-eight bucks in his wallet and a coffee can full of spare change, most of it squirreled for the next month's rent. He didn't own a car; not contributing to a carbon footprint was starting to wear on his feet and bones in what surely would degenerate into crippling arthritis.

Cute, he supposed, while checking out his face from the corners of the mirror. But there were a million other dudes just like him, horny and lost and desperate, living in Limbo while waiting for life to get better through lottery tickets and twists of fate.

What he could offer her was his cock...his *love*, and that had to count for something in a world were everyone was looking for permission to be happy.

Hugo showered, tugged another load out beneath the

spray, and dressed. His old sneakers were still wet. Not caring, he wandered out of the house in search of her.

He found the woman sitting on the sand, facing the mist-cloaked Atlantic, the pop of red color from her hair and shirt creating a bright beacon on the vacant beach. Even the surfers had abandoned the waves. The beach on this storied day was theirs alone.

"Hello," Hugo said after several attempts at talking.

The woman tipped a glance over her shoulder. "You," she said. "You're the young man who operates the carousel."

"Yes. Mind if I join you?"

The woman's eyes, so pale, so not there, dissected him. She answered with a glance at the wet sand. Hugo scrambled down beside her, high on her scent. The merry-go-round's calliope music hammered down from the direction of the amusement park.

"It's how I found it again, you know, after it vanished from the north," she said.

Hugo shrugged. "The carousel?"

"Yes, I followed the music, through the water. It makes me so happy."

A shudder tripped down Hugo's spine, curiously hot. "And riding that horse, the white one."

The woman flashed a grin filled with mystery. "You saw?"

Hugo boldly reached a hand toward her knee. "I could give you that same kind of excitement."

"Could you?" she challenged.

Hugo's fingers squeezed down. The cool, strange flesh beneath the woman's denim skirt sent strange readings pulsing through his nerves. His touch wandered higher.

"You're fucking beautiful."

He lifted her top, bared the skin beneath to the gray morning light. His fingers traveled under the woman's denim skirt, toward her sex, only—

Their lips moved together. Hugo kissed rain. Glancing down, he saw that his fingers were caressing the damp sand. There was no one on the beach.

A splashing among the waves drew Hugo's focus out to the sea, twenty feet from shore. The woman bobbed on the waves, now naked, and beckoned with the seductive curl of a finger.

Hugo stood. The calliope music from the merry-go-round slowed, warped. Splinters of light pierced the clouds, a million shards of broken mirror blinding him to the world, creating one version of reality superimposed over another.

A line of discarded clothes stretched to the water's edge, but Hugo couldn't tell if they were real. Nor did he care.

Turn around, said a voice in his thoughts. Hugo tipped a glance over his shoulder. The amusement park lurked out of focus behind the fog, but he could hear the clanking revolutions of the merry-go-round as it turned, set to the endless mad melody of calliope music. *Go back to that dragon that ate at sneakers and souls, that apartment, that nothingness.*

Hugo stripped out of his clothes and marched forward, into the ocean. Soon, the water embraced him and, showing mercy, smothered the dirge in his ears.

PATCHWORK

HOLLIE SNIDER

The convertible whispered along cracked asphalt, streaking red beneath an azure sky. Golden sunlight glinted off sand, red rock, and backyard swimming pools. Houses squatted along either side of the old highway, crowding closer together as the car approached the edge of town.

Silvi Lackmond stretched and yawned in the passenger seat, blinking sleepy eyes behind vintage, oversized sunglasses. "Where are we?"

"Just outside of town," mumbled Jonah Granger.

"Which town?" Silvi looked over at her boyfriend and brushed silver-blonde locks away from her face. Wind whipped them forward again.

He shrugged. "I dunno. A small one, I think." Jonah glanced at the houses racing by. Large stucco monstrosities with elaborate decks balanced on small lots spoke of high incomes and low privacy. "Though there seems to be money here."

Jonah slowed the car to the posted 35mph speed limit, then to 25. "Welcome to Colter Springs, Nevada," he said, reading the worn sign to the right. "Population one thousand, one hundred and eighty."

"Already?" Silvi stretched again and her stomach rumbled. "I guess the rich *have* discovered this place finally. The population went up by about a thousand. Well, I don't care how much money these new people have as long as the restaurants are still cheap and the food's still good."

"Still?" asked Jonah.

"Mmm-hmm. This is my hometown." Silvi gave him a quick kiss on the cheek. "I told you we'd be going right through it."

Tires crunched to a stop at a sand-crusted four-way intersection, and Jonah looked right then left.

"Which way do you want to go?" asked Silvi. "We have some time. I can show you around a bit."

"Which way has food?" Jonah glanced both directions again.

"Well, there's a gas station and cafe to the left, straight takes us out of town, and right is where all the housing is. That's also probably where the new shopping areas and restaurants will be."

He cranked the steering wheel and headed down the two-lane road deeper into civilization.

Ahead, he spotted a white, A-frame style building with a red roof. A large sign ran the length of the peak with "Chief Big Beef" printed in prominent letters. An image of an Indian riding a cow graced the large picture window at one end. Two older cars sat in the parking lot, while a third idled in the drive-thru.

Jonah pulled into a spot and shut off the engine. "How about here?"

Silvi opened her eyes. "The Chief Big Beef is still here? I thought it closed down."

"Guess not," he answered. "I've never seen one before, to be honest. Is this all right?"

She opened the door. "It's fine."

Jonah followed her lead, not bothering to put up the top on the convertible.

Inside, smells of hot oil, roast beef, and coffee wafted through humid, greasy air. Chromed warming lamps shone down on the counter and light glared off the branded, foil-wrapped sandwiches. Fans hung from the high ceilings, buzzing as they turned lazily. The weak effort of the blades did little to move still air. Below, booths and tables squatted in orderly rows, awaiting customers. An older couple looked up at the sound of the door chime and studied the newcomers.

Silvi ignored them, focused on the menu, but Jonah shifted under their scrutiny.

Finally, the old man and woman returned their attention to each other and Jonah relaxed. "Just get me a big sandwich, fries, and a drink," he said. "I gotta hit the head."

She nodded, still deciding on her own meal. Silvi watched Jonah walk away, waiting until the hinged door thumped shut, then hurried over to the old couple.

"What are you two doing here? I thought you understood."

The old woman touched Silvi's cheek. "We just wanted to see him, dear." Years of cigarettes graveled her voice, and she glanced at the restroom door. "He seems like a nice boy."

"He is. I really like him."

"We'll do what we can," said the old man, voice strong despite the years.

"I know." Silvi glanced over her shoulder.

"Where's he from?" The old woman picked up her sandwich. Strings of meat fell from the buttered, sesame seed bun and smacked against foil.

"Colorado."

The old woman sighed and smiled. "All right, we'll see if we can help him take Greg's place." She bit into the sandwich. "Too bad, though," she said around a mouthful. "I'd have liked to have tried Colorado. I'm tired of Utah."

"You better get back over there before he comes out." The old man grimaced at his own meal.

"Do whatever you can," Silvi begged. "Please." She strode back to the counter just as Jonah emerged.

"What can I get you, Silvi?" asked the freckled kid behind the counter.

She shushed him. "Don't use my name," she whispered.

"Oh, right. Sorry. I forgot. I'm new at this."

"Do you two know each other?" Jonah kissed Silvi's cheek.

She fumbled deep inside the purse. Hands shaking and heart pounding, Silvi pulled out the black leather billfold. "Uh, no, no."

"Oh, I thought I heard him use your name."

Silvi smiled at Jonah and placed her wallet on the counter. "You must be hearing things."

He slipped an arm around her waist. "That's possible. My ears are still plugged from the highway wind. You decide yet?"

"Yep." Silvi looked at him, gazing deep into his hazel eyes. "I know exactly what I want."

An hour and a half later, Jonah and Silvi walked further north, into Colter Springs.

"You sure it's all right to leave the car in the parking lot?" asked Jonah, glancing back.

"It's fine. Colter Springs isn't like big cities where everyone is so property possessive." Silvi squeezed his hand. "Besides, this way I can show you around better."

"Sounds good to me."

They walked hand in hand toward the smaller houses, hidden before by the larger behemoths lining the highway. Silvi pointed to the occasional house as a place she played when younger, or named friends who had lived nearby.

"See that house?" Silvi pointed to a dingy white building with peeling paint from years of sand, sun and wind. "That's where I learned to walk a tightrope. And over there," she gestured to a small pink stucco house, "is where I broke two fingers and dislocated my elbow trying to be a contortionist like Emily. She was my best friend growing up."

"Tightrope walking? Contortionist?" asked Jonah. "I played hide and seek and tag when I was a kid."

Silvi laughed. "I played those too."

The sun sank further past the horizon, casting long shadows and encouraging street lights to life.

Just ahead, a banner reading "29th Annual Colter Springs Street Carnival" stretched over the asphalt. Orange and white striped road barriers topped with flashing yellow lights blocked the road.

"Let's go check out the carnival," said Jonah. "I haven't been to one since I was little."

"I thought you had to be in Oregon the day after tomorrow for that job interview."

Jonah glanced at her. "Well, we're not gonna make it much farther tonight anyway. We can have some fun tonight, and be on the road early tomorrow. I'll still make it. Don't worry, I don't plan on screwing up that interview by being late. It's not every day I get offered my dream job! Being paid to teach others to windsurf? Come on! And Columbia Gorge is amazing. It's the windsurfing capital of the world, you know."

Silvi made a few appropriate, noncommittal sounds, having heard all about windsurfing, Columbia Gorge, and the mecca of Oregon since the phone call requesting a face-to-face interview two weeks ago.

"And when I'm not teaching, I can guide whitewater rafters and hikers eventually. Once I learn the trails and the rivers anyway. And you know how fast I can learn my way around, Silvi." Jonah looked at the banner again. "Come on. I'll win you a teddy bear. You can even name it Oregon."

She laughed and they walked past the barrier into the carnival. "I'll let you win me a bear, but naming it is up to me."

"All right. I know I've been talking about this quite a bit, and you're probably sick of it, but it's just after all the work I've put in, all the competitions and all the traveling, and keeping a day job just to survive, I can't help but be excited. It's like I'm sitting right on the edge of success and I'm finally about to fall the right way."

Silvi hugged him. "I know just how you feel."

Ringing bells and squeals echoed through the houses, growing louder as the sky darkened. Metal wheels clacked over wooden tracks as a ride picked up speed. A barker advertised his contest in a garbled voice.

"He sounds like he's eating the mike," commented Jonah. "People need to realize you don't need to be that close."

"We have a winner, winner, chicken dinner," carried through the air as an unseen player won some unidentified game.

Jonah smiled at the phrase.

All around lights flashed and noise assaulted them. Smells of buttered popcorn, toffee apples, and roasted corn filled their nostrils, making already full stomachs beg for a treat.

Silvi and Jonah passed shills carrying large stuffed animals designed to attract attention, and tents with hand-painted fabric posters advertising such things as "Pickled Punks," "the Camel Girl," and "Pumpkinhead: the Boy with Seeds for Brains."

Jonah gazed at the crude drawings of deformed human fetuses in preserving jars and a woman holding a misshapen baby with an oversized orange head. The third creation had too much wear to make out the image. People slowly queued up outside the flaps, waiting for the opportunity to cast curious, yet repulsed gazes upon the sights within.

"People really pay money to look at those things?"

Silvi shrugged. "People are morbid at heart. They want to see freaks of nature, but don't want anyone to know they want to see freaks of nature."

Along the midway, adults and children hurled wooden balls up Skee-ball tracks, cheering when they thunked into ringed pockets. Tickets spat out beneath the ball return, some faster than others. Plastic rings tinked off glass bottle necks and undersized basketballs rattled loose backstops at different games.

"Which one do you want to try?" asked Jonah.

Silvi looked around. "I'm not sure. Let's walk a little more and see the rest, then I can decide."

They passed more games, before Silvi stopped in front of an opening between two booths. She pointed. "That one."

"Shoot the freak! Shoot the freak! Come on, young

man," called the barker. "You look like someone who can shoot the freak."

Jonah looked at the game, confused.

The barker stood by a chain link fence about three feet high. Behind it, a green hedge provided a buffer between the fence and a pit decorated with barrels and bins, targets and mannequins. Weeds of various heights grew through and around the barriers. At the back, green, yellow and pink splotches from exploded paint balls splattered a graffiti-covered concrete wall. An orange, black ,and yellow sign hung just above the graffiti, announcing "Live Human Target" in letters nearly two feet tall. Cinder block and wooden shelves held dirty glass bottles, broken dolls, and assorted other stationary targets. Near the front of the pit, an old chair leaked foam through torn seams next to a scarred wooden end table.

Jonah moved closer and peered over the fence. Sunlight glinted off a person in padded pants, a helmet and large goggles. He had a leather breastplate covering his bare chest and carried a huge shield made from a flattened garbage can lid. Colored scars of red, yellow, orange, and blue from numerous past hits dotted his gear while bruises, in various states of healing, pocked tanned flesh.

The freak noticed Jonah and darted around the post-apocalyptic wasteland. He ducked behind the barrels and popped up, looking very much like a steampunk gopher.

"Didn't they close down a game like this at Coney Island in Brooklyn?" Jonah watched him for a moment, then turned toward Silvi. She shrugged.

"You want me to play this? There's not even a teddy bear for me to win."

"But it looks like fun," said Silvi. "And you might win something if you hit him."

"Shoot the freak," the barker called again at passers-by. "Step right up and shoot the freak. You could win the chance to lead our sideshow attractions in tonight's parade if you shoot the freak!"

"There you go. You could lead the parade tonight," said Silvi. She moved next to him, gazing down at the freak and his antics. "And you can still play another game and win the teddy bear."

Jonah studied the pit. "You really want me to spend money to shoot someone who's done nothing to me for a chance to lead a freak parade? What am I? An extra in a Big and Rich video?"

Silvi laughed, linking her arm through Jonah's, and winked at the barker. "This is the one," she said.

The barker winked back.

"All right," said Jonah, "I'll try. But I'm not a very good shot." He pulled out his wallet and turned to the barker. "How much?"

"Five dollars," he answered. "Five dollars to shoot the freak five times."

Jonah handed the bill over.

"What color would you like?" asked the barker, voice increasing in volume. "I'd recommend green. It's seems to be a more accurate color."

Jonah took the paintball rifle offered to him. "How can on color be more—no, no I don't want to know. Just give me the green ones."

The barker fit a hopper with five balls in it onto the top of the gun. "Now, just aim and pull the trigger."

Jonah sighted in on the man in the pit, expecting him to jump around.

The freak stood centered between two barrels, waiting.

"Is he gonna move?"

The barker peered over the fence. "What do you mean? He's moving all over the place."

Jonah looked back. The freak stood stock still, staring up at them.

"You've paid your money, young man. No refunds. Are you going to shoot him or not? I don't know how much longer he can keep up that level of activity."

Jonah glanced at Silvi, sighed, and squeezed the trigger.

Thwap!

The first paintball splattered against padded pants just above the left knee.

Thwap! Thwap! Twang!

Two more hit the freak's body and one hit the shield.

"Great job! One more shot, young man," encouraged the barker. "Make it count."

"Aim for the head," said Silvi. "If you shoot him in the head, I bet you win."

Jonah lined the freak's head up in the sights, and lowered the weapon slightly before pulling the trigger one last time. The paintball spun, arcing toward the freak's chest. He sighed in relief.

Then the freak ducked.

Green paint splattered against the helmet and the freak fell backwards into the dirt. He lay still.

Jonah stared at the unmoving form in shock. "How," he began. "I wasn't even aiming for his head. I was aiming for his chest. Did I kill him?"

The freak rolled over and stood, brushing dust off his pants. He gave Jonah a thumbs-up and vanished behind a sheet hanging over the back wall.

Jonah handed the weapon back to the barker. "But I don't want to lead your parade."

The barker took the gun and hung it on a rack next to

two others. "I told you, green seems to be a more accurate color." He put his arm around Jonah's shoulder, ignoring Jonah's statement. "Now, it's time to get you ready."

"Silvi," called Jonah.

"I'm coming." She hurried to his side and grabbed his hand. "I'm coming too."

"Now, Silvi," said the barker. "You know you can't be with him for this."

"I know. But I can walk him to the tent."

Jonah looked from the barker to Silvi and back. "Do you two know each other? What's going...?" He tried to plant his feet on the cracked asphalt, but the barker simply pushed him harder, forcing Jonah to walk in halting steps.

"It's all right, Jonah. Mister Brandson's daughter and I went to school together. I told you about Emily. She's the contortionist. Remember?"

Jonah nodded, confusion coloring his face. "What's going on here, Silvi?"

"They're going to make it where you don't have to go to that job interview. Where I don't have to go to Oregon and live in the cold. We can be together and happy traveling the country and seeing the sights. This is the first carnival of the year for us, start of the season. We perform for the locals and tourists passing through, then on to other cities for the rest of the summer, before returning to winter quarters in Colter Springs. You can have a job right here and live with us. "

"Us? What do you mean, *us*?"

They arrived at a brightly colored tent. Electric white lights flickered in a string around the entrance. "I'll wait right here for you," she promised.

"What do you mean, *us*?" he called again. "I need to get to that interview. Come on. Joke's over. You had your fun."

The barker pulled back the tent flap, keeping one hand on Jonah's shoulder.

"Silvi?"

Inside, Silvi glimpsed a sheet-draped table, gleaming surgical tools arrayed neatly on a rolling metal tray and several disposable coolers distinctly marked with red biohazard symbols. A hump-backed woman with knees and elbows bending the opposite direction nature intended held up a hypodermic needle, examining the fluid level in the reservoir.

"Silvi!" Jonah planted his feet as the contents captured his attention. "No! No, no, no. I am *not* going in there." He jerked away from the barker and took a few running steps before being stopped by a strongman wearing only cut-off overalls.

"Gigantis," said the barker, "if you would please escort Jonah into the tent."

The strongman wrapped his arms around Jonah and lifted the smaller man off his feet.

"Let me go! Silvi!" Jonah twisted his body, fighting against the steel grip of Gigantis. "Silvi!"

The flap dropped with a whoosh, muffling further protests.

Silvi stood outside for a few moments, listening to low, unintelligible murmurs. A sharp "No" ricocheted through the slightly open canvas doorway, followed by clanging metal and stifled curses. A scream, ragged and raw, ripped through the night, then silence, uncomfortable in its suddenness.

"I told you not to fight, Jonah." Silvi shook her head and turned away to walk the grounds.

She bought a toffee apple at the closest grab joint, crunching through the entire treat, stick and all, then proceeded to eat a second, followed by a third as she meandered. Lights flickered in the dark now and stars twinkled above. Hot dogs added their salty aroma to the carnival smells as they were placed on grills for the evening offerings.

Two of the cooks, one a woman Silvi barely knew, strode by. A metal bucked squeaked in her hands, dripping red behind it. "Looks like we'll be eating leftovers tonight, instead of Colorado-grown."

The other grunted, thrusting his head in Silvi's direction by way of a greeting. The two hurried toward the mess tent, flanked by two hopping and leaping children each about seven years old.

The kids grabbed at the chunks of raw meat with grubby fingers. "Please," the boy barked. "Don't cook it."

"We like it wrrraaaaahhh," croaked in the girl. Sunglasses slipped to her nose, revealing oversized golden eyes with horizontal pupils. "Tastes betterrrrrrrrrrr. Coooooooooooked is no good." She pushed the glasses up and hiccupped as she leapt forward again.

"Yeah, wrah." The boy squawked. "Cooked is no gooooooood."

"No good, no good." They sing-songed back and forth in wheezing harmony, circling the two adults as they walked.

One of the children grabbed at the bucket again, wrapping fingers around the rim and earning a stinging slap.

He wailed and shook the injured hand, then resumed snatching at the contents with his cohort.

Silvi laughed at the antics of the Frog Children and waved to workers as she passed, calling out greetings to some and responding to others.

"Hey," called another carny. "You're back."

She stopped and smiled. "I am, Claw. And I think I found someone to take over for Greg. He's in the tent right now." Silvi studied the game behind the carny. A painted wooden clown stood, gaping colored mouth awaiting weighted bags to be tossed down his gullet. Above, plush bears, dogs, horses, and cats swung in the gentle breeze that had picked up. She moved closer, intent on a white bear with a black human face.

"See one you like?" he asked.

She pointed. "I like that one."

Claw turned and looked. He reached up and grabbed the bear's leg with a pincered hand. "Then that's the one he'll win for you later."

"Hey, you did a good job earlier, letting Jonah hit you so easily."

Claw blushed. "Thanks. It was hard just standing there, but you signaled he was the one, so I did it."

Silvi glanced at her watch, noting nearly four hours had passed. "I'd better get back. He'll be up soon. I'll see you later?"

Claw nodded and tucked the bear under the counter, out of sight from the other marks wandering the carnival.

"Hey, do you have anything to eat back there?" she asked, turning back to Claw.

"Nah, nothing but a few bottles of water. We've all taken to putting our food over by the petting zoo. Safer than storing it near the mess tent."

"Yeah, that's right. Parts of our lunches were ending up in food for marks. I remember. Thanks. I'll go by there."

Claw nodded and Silvi waved farewell.

She strode back toward the large tent, cutting around game stands and food carts, hoping to arrive in time to at least give the appearance she had waited for Jonah like she promised. But the petting zoo, and the opportunity for a quick snack, beckoned.

"Hi, Paul," she greeted the man at the gate to the white-fenced corral.

Inside miniature goats, donkeys, rabbits and pot-bellied pigs withstood the onslaught of ear-pulling and eye-poking with lazy patience. Children squealed with delight as oblivious parents watched with bemused expressions.

Silvi grinned at the money changing hands, fueled by kids demanding to feed the animals. "Looks like business is good."

The thin, balding man turned to face her, eyes bulging from their cavernous sockets. Sunken cheeks and a sallow complexion added to the disturbing sight.

"Save it for the show, Pop-Eye," Silvi said, using his stage name as a reminder. "Claw said you have real food here. I need a quick snack, if you have something. I'm on my way back to see how Jonah's doing."

Paul nodded and blinked, eyes retreating to their proper place. Wordlessly, he handed her a small paper lunch sack. The base sagged, making a crinkling noise as she took it.

"Thanks. See you later?"

He nodded again, turning his attention back to the petting zoo. Paul gave a little girl about three years old a toothless grin as a rabbit hopped into her lap. She screamed with laughter and stroked its long ears.

Silvi's stomach rumbled and she cast a look of longing at the girl and the bunny, then turned away. She carried her bag toward the tent housing Jonah. With one hand, she reached in and removed a peeping brown and yellow chick. Darting her gaze about, Silvi looked for anyone who might see, then stretched her jaw wide. She popped the protesting bird into her mouth and bit down. Fluid dribbled from her chin as the chick gave a startled squawk before Silvi swallowed. She wiped her chin and pulled out a second chick.

This one settled in the warmth of her hand, eyes closed, breathing comfortable and regular. The rapid heartbeat pulsed against her palm.

Silvi tossed the paper bag in a garbage bin as she passed. She stroked the downy head, letting her fingers glide along the velvety baby softness. The chick stirred, shifting its feet and fluttering its wings. The eyes remained closed and it soon quieted again.

Silvi opened her jaw wider than for the last snack, and she placed the chick on her still reddened tongue. The bird peeped one, twice, then, feeling the warmth, snuggled down. Silvi closed her teeth gently, memorizing the feel of the tiny feet on her tongue, the fuzz against the roof of her mouth, the small breaths against her teeth. Blood, coppery and hot, washed along her throat as Silvi chewed. Bones snapped and cracked, piercing gums and tongue. Silvi relished the stinging pain. Nearly a month had passed since she'd had real food, and her stomach growled with the pleasure of it.

She swallowed and wiped her mouth on her shirt-sleeve, making a mental note to find Paul later and thank him again.

The tent flap pulled back just as Silvi reached it. Light flowed out, coloring the ground in gold. Jonah stood haloed by the glow, an angry gaze trained on her face.

"Y—you...you thaid you'd wait right heeah," he mumbled. Words formed with difficulty from a misshapen jaw and a trickled of blood oozed from the corner of his mouth. "Wh–where were you?"

Silvi stepped forward.

Irregular patches of new skin covered Jonah's body. Black, bronzed red, tattooed, and creamy white all held together with thick, colored thread of reds, silver, blues, pinks, greens and golds. His bare, stitched chest rose and fell with even breaths, metallic strands glinting with the movements. Ragged jeans hugged his hips, stitches disappearing beneath the material only to reappear at the tattered hems just below his knees. Bare feet shifted on the asphalt. Toes, now irregular in size and length, wiggled against the rough surface. Blood wept from dark sutures and the left pinky toenail gleamed hot pink. A hypodermic needle protruded from the corner of his left eye, leftover liquid sloshing in the reservoir with each blink.

"Silvi," said the old woman from the restaurant. "You did it." She smiled and touched Jonah's shoulder. "You've brought us a new Patchwork Man."

Jonah shrugged away from the old woman and spread his arms. Sutures puckered and pulled at the skin. Clear fluid and darker blood trickled from the wounds. Drops pocked against packed earth. "Ju—just look what they did. What they did when you were gone." Words began to form easier for him though his chest heaved with the effort. "Look what they did!" Laughter rasped and whistled from his mangled body. "Look what they did," he repeated, softer now. "Look what they did to me." Tears trailed along the metal shaft still imbedded in one eye and dripped to the ground with little plashing noises. Jonah fell to his knees.

Stitches tore around the joints, rending sensitive flesh. He stared up at Silvi, fear and longing evident. He hiccuped and giggled. "Look." He pushed the needle deeper into his eye and pressed the plunger, injecting the last of the clear yellow fluid.

Silvi stepped forward and knelt in front of him. Gingerly, she pulled the hypodermic free and handed it up.

"Look at that," said Gigantis, holding the syringe up. "She pulled the sword from the stone. Guess we have a new king to lead the parade tonight." He guffawed at his joke, eliciting a few snickers and murmurs of agreement.

Jonah winced and teetered on his knees. Blood ran in rivulets from his jaw, shoulders, and chest.

"Patch," Silvi breathed, wrapping her arms around his neck. "You're beautiful." She steadied his rocking and kissed his sutured, mismatched lips. "So beautiful."

EMPLOYEE OF THE MONTH

E. F. SCHRAEDER

Lakeside Beach Park tickets were on sale everywhere. After notching out a meager existence for more than fifty years, the spotty park attendance depended on locals who needed the regular bargains, discounts, and specials to draw ever shrinking crowds to the battered wooden rides and impossible to win games. The surrounding Lakeside community looked almost as dingy as the run-down park at the end of the season.

Outside of a handful of tragic accidents, the park was well regarded by local customers. Even those tragedies were swallowed into the park's nostalgia, and they now devoted private tours to a handful of ghost hunters and psychics. *Group rates made a killing. Any publicity was good publicity.* Aria learned that night four of training.

Despite its shortcomings, Lakeside Beach Park inspired a certain degree of community pride. That's why Aria's mom encouraged her to work there, thinking she'd make some new connections and a little decent cash for college.

This year's opening special promised two free children admittance with two adult ticket purchases. Aria purchased the two adult tickets as a gift for her mom and boyfriend, who had a six-year-old son of his own. She figured he'd bring a friend.

"Got you these," Aria said, waving the tickets.

"Sweetie, you're already doing such a great job! Look at you supporting the park. I bet you were the first employee to buy tickets this year!"Aria's mother beamed.

Aria wriggled out from beneath an attempted hug and squinted her dark eyes up at her mother. Aria offered a half smile, blowing it off. "Steve said we should get tickets for free to keep people coming, but only upper management gets them."

"He sounds like a real troublemaker," her mom said.

"He's my boss. Well, one of my bosses. I'm pretty low on the ladder." Aria handed her the tickets. "You guys should visit me if I'm on that day. I'll give the swings extra speed." Aria grinned, feeling a little proud and a little embarrassed about having so little to show for herself. She hoped to earn enough cash to help her get out of this crappy town soon. Aria tucked a stray wisp of frazzled blonde hair behind her ear and headed off for her last night of training.

"That's right, hon. Don't be late for work. Sets a bad example. See you tonight." Her mom blew a kiss. She watched Aria's petite frame hustle to the beat-up sedan. Aria still looked too young to drive, let alone join the local workforce. A surge of pride swelled to see her daughter take on her first real job. Even if it was at that crusty old park. It was something. Enough. "Don't worry about getting home early, either. Go have fun with your friends from work," she added as a hopeful smile crossed her face. "Except that Steve character, you look out for him." She smiled wearily, then blew Aria another kiss.

Aria waved goodbye, arm dangling out of the car window, without knowing she wouldn't see her mom later. Or ever again.

Aria was completely tired of the dull training sessions. One night to go. Sigh. Did she really have to understand park politics to flip the switch on the high swings?

HR Man explained the economics with a flat tone and expressionless face. "Ticket costs are kept relatively low, management counts on profits from customer spending. Wholesale popcorn is cheap and irresistible once customers inhale the buttery scent. Yes, we pump the scent into the midway." He smiled. "Every kernel popped is a job saved," he told the new recruits. From the back row of the room, Aria couldn't help but roll her eyes.

Ever since Lakeside Park developed a reputation for violating labor laws, their human resource manager worked pretty hard on sounding like they cared when talking to recruits. Sounding like they cared was cheaper than lawsuits.

"OMG bored," Aria texted her mom, who didn't text back "pay attn," but Aria knew that's what she'd say. Aria forced herself to sit up straight and concentrate on the droning voice coming from the front of the room. *Got it. Upsells are the key for frivolous souvenirs, food concessions, and useless memorabilia.* She yawned.

"Kitsch trends and retro fads dominated, and sienna tinted old west photos fuel the bottom line...."

Aria made a mental note: *Popcorn sells like crack. Remember: Studies show that people in the Midwest will buy food almost anywhere.* The air at Lakeside already smelled like hot oil and pavement. *How is that even possible?*

Aria brushed up on park history during a break. She leafed through the training manual instead of chatting to the other new hires. They all seemed to know each other. She ignored them when they glanced her way, burying her face into the manual as if it was the latest bestseller.

Aria read carefully. Attaining status as a historical park was practically the sole thing that kept them afloat, making them a candidate for a spike of news articles every season that attracted guests hungry for old time charm. *Lakeside peddled old charm better than the rest of them. No new rides equaled no new construction cost, no new signs, no new upper level staff. Quaint was free, everything else you paid for at Lakeside.* She felt like an expert already, and at only 18.

The historical status even helped management acquire a handful of state grants trickle in to help with maintenance and repairs. Everything fit neatly in place and kept Lakeside floating above foreclosure. Every summer they managed to pull in a few local kids to work. It was necessary for their mediocre survival, and attracting young workers was simple. The park needed cheap workers, like Aria, who thought park employment sounded fun. Well, better than fast food. *Like giving babies work as diaper testers, Lakeside knew where to put its shit jobs.*

Aria looked out the window at the faded whitewash on the fence around the park. It matched the overall gray tint of the faded rides, long past due for fresh paint. But antiques didn't need to be refurbished. Everything seemed smudged with a layer of grease and grime, soiled from years of use. Even the food carts, which apparently met some basic quality standard, looked grungy, just sitting amidst all the other junk. She watched Steve tying flags together with long black cords he pulled out of his pockets. It looked like a magic trick with unending knots and strings.

Class dismissed. Aria headed over to the rides crew, already hanging outside behind the rotten looking fence. She was the only new hire slotted for ride work. Lucky her.

"I know a really good one," Carlotta said, "and this one's really true." She squatted down in front of the picnic table with the other employees on break. Her blue smock bunched around her torso as she knelt awkwardly toward Kevin's lighter to flare up a cig. Dark hair framed Carlotta's face as she took a long pull, then exhaled until smoke swirled around her. Her deep brown eyes looked serious and her voice was a little hoarse.

"They're all true, Carly," Steve interrupted.

Carly continued over the crew's laughter, "In nineteen forty-four, during the war, Lakeside almost closed after some kids died up on the Ferris wheel. One of them dared the other to stand up when they were at the very top," Carly stood up on tip toe. She wobbled and stretched her arms overhead to act out the tragedy, in the process exposing a flat, well-tanned stomach and a gold hoop piercing in her belly button. Steve hooted at her, but she pressed on over him, "And when he did, the bench teetered over, whoosh! They both tumbled right out, all the way to the beach. Broke their necks." She made a snapping sound, clicking her mouth. Finished, Carly tapped a long ash from her cigarette. Carly spun on her heel to make eye contact with everyone, contorting her expression into pain and wrenching her neck so it looked out of joint. She had a flair for the dramatic.

The park was full of dead people, if they told it right. Gray-eyed corpses behind every rigged ring toss game

147

and heaps of broken bodies beneath rickety, repaired wooden coasters. Park legends accounted for crashes, fights, and random incidents. Every tale spun filled Lakeside with decades of a sordid, gory history. No wonder about the ghost hunter tours. Warm blood spilled and dried, crusted over like the flaking paint; necks snapped; angry parents protesting the decisions of a reckless management. None of it amounted to much more than fodder for the rumor mill after all this time.

And Lakeside Beach Park loved its rumors. They traveled faster than most of the old coasters. A fender bender in the parking lot before 9AM opening, and the employees would chatter about it all day. Add something with a bit of gore and gruesome, and it became legend.

"No way, that's nothing compare to the old woman, the one who drowned—"

"Aww, the one they tried to revive under the swings? Not that one again," Steve interrupted, shoving Kevin aside. He kicked at the wall mindlessly, "Hey Darius, how long do we have?"

"Under the swings?" Aria asked, her dark eyes wide. Aria just received her assignment, and was initially glad to operate the swings. Suddenly the thought of some bloated body sputtering its last breaths where she'd tromp around to make college cash gave her a chill. No one seemed to be listening to her. Aria's large eyes blinked at them, but her question remained unanswered.

Carly leaned over to Aria, whispering in her ear, "Yes, those swings...your swings." Aria shuddered as Carlotta filled in the blanks, "She'd been looking for her daughter at the beach, but...." She stuck her tongue out and made a gagging face and choking sound. *Again with the dramatics.* Aria sighed. "They pulled her out but couldn't revive her." Carlotta watched Aria's eyes harden, then added,

"Hey, at least she didn't croak *on* the swings, right?" She smiled, nudging Aria's shoulder.

Aria forced a smile and swallowed hard, nervously listening to the old timers talk trash about the park. Her eyes darted to each member of the much older than her crew, all of them seemed to be experts on local gore. She noticed her stomach suddenly ached a little. *Maybe HR training was better than socializing.*

A long peal of recorded barbershop quartet singing began as management tried out the new sound system. Rides cranked and creaked, springing into action around them as they were tested and retested for opening day. It seemed funny, everything operational now at night though the park was empty. Organ tunes piped and chimed in a steady rhythm up from the nearby carousel as it spun into action. The music whirred at a steady, quick pace that matched the ride's speed. The gang glanced over at the merry-go-round. Aria eyed the plaster horses galloping nowhere in a hurry, their ears perpetually flattened back, mouths in aggressive snarls, and nostrils flared as if in the throes of the Kentucky Derby.

"Break's up in five," Darius, their manager announced, rising from the picnic table and heading back toward his post. The heavy wooden door swung shut with a thud after him. Darius had a goal. The crew opened tomorrow, and he didn't want them to get used to goofing off before opening. He flung the uniform smock over his shoulder and flipped his thick dreadlocks behind one ear, shaking his head. He hated listening to them get superstitious, but it happened every year. Employee antics were almost as predictable as the clicking of a coaster before it sped downhill.

Darius looked around the old park with a smug grin, unsurprised that it could conjure up fear in the new recruits. This was a dreary place on a sunny day. No matter how many times shit got repainted, peeling grayish blue paint reappeared on the rides and displays, the old fashioned decorations testaments to an era of burlesque thrills and carnival sideshows. Freaks, castoffs, and runaways populated the place every season with a fresh crop of employees. Some people returned every summer, and Lakeside always found a way to welcome them all. Every year. Darius had been here longer than any of them. To him it felt like home; he was just another one of the haunted.

Steve voiced up, "What about the car that derailed on Scorpio back in nineteen-fifty-four?" His turn to tell a tale, he knew the routine. The Scorpio accident was Steve's favorite story. "Scorpio was a new ride that year, and a huge draw for the park. It was eight stories high, a record for the park back then, and a towering feat of curves and hills that was unlike any coaster in the country. The ride was packed the entire opening weekend, forty minute lines, setting records for speed. All the while the park tallied up tickets and cash like never before.

"Scorpio required investors, and investors expected to get paid. The third weekend, the park still overflowed with a buzz. The white and red striped uniforms of soda jerks still fresh and crisp, first of the season, and everyone was enthralled with the prospect of Lakeside's success, like they'd turned a corner."

Everyone but Aria, who was the newest hire, knew the story, but they still hung on Steve's every word. He had a knack for telling this one. Aria shivered. Her small mouth hung open and dark eyes widened. Aria brushed a hand through her thick hair, and it bristled into a frizzy yellow twist as she twirled it mindlessly, captivated by Steve's story.

"Too much run time. That's what they figured after it happened. But on the third weekend, after running non-stop, one of the cars caught loose at the top of the big hill." Steve pointed, the peak of the coaster visible on the edge of the park. "It unhinged and toppled off the track, wheels wobbling and screams filling the air. Hardly anyone noticed it over the general mayhem of the park, of course. Everyone screams here," he added with a sinister smile. "Killed six people. Four in the car." He paused dramatically, "plus the two they landed on," he pointed to the crash site below.

"Ewww! That's gross!" Aria's face crumbled and pulled her eyes away from the ride as its empty cars clicked wearily up the hill on a test ride. Aria swallowed hard and tried to act nonchalant, but she felt she was already getting a reputation as being inexperienced. The baby of the bunch. Aria wrinkled her nose, resentment already building about being the youngest in the rides crew. Lips pouting in a very childish pose, Aria hurried to think up something clever to say. "They should put up a memorial or something...all that death."

Aria was eighteen going on twelve if life experience had anything to do with it. She was cute in a petite girl sort of way, like a pixie. Aria always wore baggy clothes that swallowed her whole and left her looking even tinier. An oversized mop of thick yellow hair hid much of Aria's face unless it was pulled back, which revealed dark, big eyes. Aria didn't like hearing about accidents and death, though she tried to hide her squeamishness. She felt too naive to be a part of the regular crew.

"Not this company," Carlotta said flatly. "Lose too

much revenue, scare people off. They keep the death chasers on private tours. They cover up as much as they can, sister. Don't you forget it. You watch your back, eh? They hear you talking like that and you'll disappear quick." She snickered, tucking a strand of black hair behind her ear.

"Disap– what do you mean?" Aria snapped her head round to look straight at Carlotta.

"Fire you, hon. Not kill you," Carlotta replied calmly, pulling her dark hair into a tight pony tail with a thick fabric band.

"That's what you think," Steve added, chuckling and scratching the reddish blond stubble on his chin. Steve squinted at Aria, noticing how squeamish she was and wondering how long she'd last.

"Okay kids, time to get back to set up." Darius returned, knotting the smock behind his back. He tucked his braids into a neat loop that swung while he walked toward them. "We've got a lot to finish up before tomorrow." It was true.

Beside the vendor cart selling popcorn and pretzels a six foot plaster clown stood, a thick wide red grin painted fresh on its mouth and a stiff lot of felt park flags for sale clutched in his oversized, outstretched hands. "Buy one get one free" a little painted sign said in front of him.

"Who would want two of them?" Aria asked Carly, pointing at the crappy felt Lakeside flags. She hoped her sarcasm would yield her a little slack in the unpopularity contest she seemed to be winning.

"Got me." Carly laughed.

"I got two. Hanging over my bed," Steve said, flicking the flags. The flags moved in a stiff back and forth, jerked motion from their wire extensions as Steve flicked them with his thick, stubby fingers.

God he's gross, Aria thought. *I've got to get out of rides.*

"Now right there," Darius pointed at the clown, "is an ideal employee. Never late, always dressed in uniform, always smiling. Makes money, and he doesn't take anything off payroll." He slapped the hollow clown's shoulder like it was an old pal.

Steve patted the clown's ass, adding, "And no sexual harassment claims from missy clown pants."

"Or mister clown pants...I've never checked, Steve, have you?" Darius offered the silent clown a warm smile, then patted Steve on the shoulder, nudging him along. "We don't want anyone scared into a complaint before we open the damned park, right Steve?" Darius kept pushing Steve ahead.

Aria smiled at Darius. If Steve was revving up his attitude, she hoped like hell Darius would intervene.

"Creepy," Aria muttered.

Darius returned a careful smile.

"No clown fearing allowed here, sweetie," Carlotta whispered in her ear with a wink.

"Carly, have any, um," Aria started, pulling a black hooded sweatshirt around herself and zipped it up to her chin.

"What?" Carly kept walking.

Aria struggled to keep up with Carly's pace. She noticed that even Carly's long stride seemed infinitely cooler than her own little short-legged strut. She glanced up at Carly, who was at least four inches taller than her. "Have employees...uh, died here?" Aria finished. She gulped hard, immediately wishing she hadn't asked anything so stupid. So obvious. Her eyes widened as she looked at Carly.

Carlotta shrugged. "Probably. Sure, kid. We'd be the last to know."

Steve fell back intentionally and stepped between

Aria and Carly. "Hey, girls." He extended his long arms over their shoulders. "Look out rides, it's go time!" he announced, trying to cheer the mood he'd dampened with his unwelcome antics and stories. He figured Darius would give him shit for it later, setting a bad tone as supervisor. He squeezed their shoulders, even the new girl. Whatever. He didn't really care. It was fun to scare the newbies.

Opening weekend in May, the sky was bright blue, but the air crisp. The weather could turn cold at any minute, the downside of its location on the Great Lakes. The employees layered up, since they technically didn't have to be in full uniform today.

Aria wore a blue pair of long johns under a pair of long black shorts and a black hooded zip up sweatshirt over the blue "Lakeside" smock with the white swirl of wave and logo emblazoned on it. Yesterday she trained all day to run the high swings. A simple enough duty, but now that she'd heard about all the accidents and had more than enough teasing from Steve, she thought about transferring to food service. Popcorn sounded good. She liked popcorn. What had the hiring manager told recruits? *A kernel popped is a job saved? Catchy. Even if it was greasier work and less pay.*

Aria, Steve, and Carly walked down the midway of the park together until Aria wriggled out of Steve's clingy grasp. She eyed every detail. Bright royal blue and white plastic flags framed the archways of every entrance and flipped noisily in the wind. Spotlights trained on the ride signs cast a bright, upward light that made them shimmer.

"Sounds like they're about to break loose and flap through the park," Aria said, pointing at them while they flipped.

"No way, I tied 'em. Nothing breaks out of my knots, baby," he said, glancing at Aria. He pulled out a handful of the remaining black cords from the pouch pocket of his sweatshirt and waved them at her.

Aria didn't smile back. *Seriously, I'm going to report him. Does he think he's flirting? Could I report flirting? Maybe he'd back off if I ignore him.* She was half his age at least. *Bondage? Really?* She shivered, stepping closer to Carly.

"Just 'cause she's blonde, doesn't mean she's your blow up doll, Steve. Give it a rest. This is the part of the movie where you get slapped," Carlotta snapped. Aria smiled a grateful thanks in her direction. "Maybe you should give that clown your action," she added crisply.

"Ouch. Aiight, hear you. I'm backing up." Steve raised his arms in the air then chimed, "Beep beep beep," while he took several steps back.

Bet he's used to taking steps backwards, Aria thought, chuckling to herself.

During training week the town felt as empty as the park. Aria remembered her training. Light tourism fed the shriveling local economy, and before the park opened everything else stayed closed. In theory, the rickety wooden rides perched on a prime piece of real estate, with nearly 1,000 feet of lakefront frontage. But big entertainment companies ignored the independent parks; the little ones like Lakeside were poor investments. They were too small to bother with, no competition at all. That mindset left employees with few opportunities to move up even if they were interested in the industry. Mostly employees were left with nothing to do but stay here and wait for reopening.

He's going nowhere fast, just like the merry-go-round, Aria thought. She was right. That's what happened with

Steve. Started as a summer gig. Ten years later he was still stuck there in a dead end job. Aria glanced at him again, barely hiding her grin. *What a loser. See if I'm still stuck here in ten years.*

Steve's years were a blur to him. He earned plenty and had no reason to leave, his time at Lakeside an even split between blackouts and paychecks. Who was this bitch to judge? Hell, working half a year was better than anything. Darius was the only one who'd here longer than Steve, and he had too much responsibility to have any fun. Steve liked his job just the way it was. Drunk or stoned most nights and half the days, Steve kept himself entertained teasing the fresh crop of hires until the jokes were flatter than roadkill.

Steve squinted, staring at Aria until his eyes narrowed sharply. A cruel expression hung on his face, as if he'd read her sarcastic thoughts. He stepped toward her, and she instinctively backed away. In his pocket, he thumbed the black cords and dimly imagined her pouting little mouth with a tight fist stuffed inside it.

Steve waved an arm over toward the rusted metal skeleton figurines dancing a jig in front of a wooden shanty. One skeleton sat in a motion automated rocking chair, its mechanical foot stomped in time with the music that blared through the hidden speakers. Steve pointed at them and shoved Aria on the back. "There's some dead employees over there...they started in nineteen-twenty. Never left." He cackled.

"Just a few years before you, huh Steve?" Carlotta snapped. She clapped a hand on Aria's shoulder adding, "He's our supervisor. He's an ass. Ignore him. Listen to Darius."

Steve hid a smoldering glance at Carly and Aria, turning his back to them. He'd get the last laugh. No doubt about that.

Aria smiled, happy to be making a pal with Carlotta. Everyone seemed to like Carly a lot. Aria walked over to the swings and started checking the belts. She let out a gasp when she saw what looked like an old woman, sitting in one of the rides.

"What the?" Aria broke off, rubbing her eyes. When she looked back, no one sat there. Of course no one was there. The park was closed. No guests until tomorrow, but that old woman had been as clear as anything. When Aria arrived closer to the swing, she reached out a hand. Aria inspected the spot where she'd seen the old woman and noticed something like a puddle beneath the seat. Aria rubbed her eyes again, and sweat beaded up on her face. She nudged the liquid with her foot and looked up, checking for leaks. It wasn't oil, though. Just water. It seemed a weird texture, though. *Strange. Real strange.* Then she blinked it out of her mind.

"See a ghost, Aria?" Steve shouted over to her from the whirling tea cups. Yep, she'd get hers.

Steve revved the tea cups, which cranked and spun until the sound alone was almost enough to make Aria feel nauseated. Aria didn't look up at Steve. She shook her head and refused to make eye contact. He stood watching her, silently wringing his hands, as an absent, angry glare filled his eyes.

She figured he'd done something, rigged it up to freak her out. He really was an ass. All that talk about park victims and cover-ups. It left plenty to the imagination as she looked around the old place. No, she didn't like Steve, and she didn't want to work with him, especially not at closing. Not at night. No telling what he'd pull.

Aria walked back to the swings for a second run. Had to make sure it wasn't the ride. She eyed it as the swing seats rose into the cool evening air, with smells of dead fish rising from the lake. She watched the empty nylon safety straps flap as they whirled around, strapped to no one. Of course. No sign of any problem.

Except that one seat, as she watched, seemed to move in a distinct pattern. Her eyes were unable to focus because of the speed of the thing, but one seat didn't look empty. She made out only a dim gray face in a blur as it whirled past again. Instinct caused her to step back, but she watched closely for it to reappear. Then spotted it, almost spectral, mouth contorted in an agony of expression. It couldn't be real. It had sullen, dark eyes and bloated, puffy features. Like it had drowned. Aria moved toward the brake, lowered her hand to it without taking her eyes away from the awful sight. Then as it rounded nearer again its mouth widened into a terrible, sickening smile.

Aria's stomach fluttered as she watched it spin around and around, eyeing her. Aria watched it cycle out of control, unaware the ride was spinning faster than it should until it made her dizzy to watch.

Aria clutched the brake and brought the swings to a slower pace, but fear rippled through her. "It's nothing," she told herself, stiffening her resolve. "There's nothing there." She felt a wet clasp on her shoulder and shrieked, then muffled back a faint cry. "Get yourself together," Aria muttered to herself. "It's just a breeze."

Aria made the request official after cleaning up her area for the night, walking up to Darius. The park was so quiet it was eerie, and she quickened her pace to get to him. "Hey, I don't want to make a big deal or anything, but do you guys, Steve maybe, prank the newcomers? There was this puddle that kept reappearing." She cut herself off, not wanting to talk about what else she'd seen. "I feel like I'm getting the raw end of a bargain, like maybe I'm going to get a hard time around here."

Darius nodded, agreed, and did his best to reassure her. He called Steve to him on the walkie talkie then watched her walk back to her station and noticed how slowly she approached the ride. Her small strides hesitated then paused. She glanced to the swings and stopped, almost as if she were talking to someone. But, of course, no one was there. Not really. Not that anyone else could see, at least.

"No way, man. She won't last long if she can't take a joke." Steve defensively snorted, fully enthralled with his efforts at hazing the new girl, as usual.

"Oh, she'll be here a while." Darius nodded in her direction. A muffled sound hung in the air as they listened to the swings start up again. "D'you even know what you're doing?" he asked, genuinely convinced that Steve had no clue knew how malicious he seemed to the kid.

"She just didn't show?" Steve asked flatly.

"Nope. Nothing. Never made it home. Her mom called looking for her last night. I was still here, of course, pulling a late one, you know. A lot to do before today. She's just gone. Dumb kid. I guess her car was still in the lot and everything. Park's going to want to hush this one for sure. Cops everywhere this morning. Already towed her car out, searching for signs of struggle. Hell, there's no sign she got that far. All they found was her sweatshirt strapped into the swing, drenching wet. Then nothing. Like she just vanished. Thin air." Darius waved his hands near his head and eyed Steve, wary of Aria's nervousness around him. A fact he'd alluded to when interviewed by the cops. That was Steve's problem, now.

"Sucked into Lakeside legend after a week of training. Gotta be a record, huh?" Steve asked, smiling. "Guess we need to pop some popcorn. An employee saved, you know...." He laughed.

"Yah," Darius shrugged, uneasy. In addition to being a real tragedy, her disappearance would screw up scheduling for a few weeks. They walked by the plaster clown, and neither of them noticed the dark puddle at its feet.

THE GOD BOX

DAVID HEATH

CONEY ISLAND POLICE REPORT

DATE: March 26th, 1945

SCENE OF CRIME: Half Sun Hotel, Room 65, 239 West Winster St.

SUSPECTED CRIME: Suicide / No foul play suspected

VICTIM: Bill Hitchens
Description of Crime Scene: Victim found with apparent self-inflicted gunshot wound through the mouth; hotel room otherwise undisturbed; Victim DOA

INVENTORY: 1 pack of chewing gum / pistol, automatic; M1911 .45 cal / wallet; 13 dollars cash; 1 state ID (Georgia) / audio recording, wax

::: BEGIN PLAYBACK :::

"If yer hearing this message, then I reckon I've bitten the dust and I'm already up in Heaven with the God Almighty. I'm hopin' that my body here won't cause too much of a hassle to clean up, 'cause I was never one to want to cause a fuss fer no one. And before you go thinkin' it, I know that a grown man killin' himself ought to be considered a sin, but I need you to hear me out first. There ain't no way I can reconcile what I done with who I am now, an' this is the only way I'm gonna find even a little bit a peace with myself. This recording I'm makin' here ain't to try and get sympathy or forgiveness for the pain I caused, but it's more a way for me to try and stop them voices in my head that remind me every day of what I done. I can hear 'em right now, yapping in my ears, tryin' to convince me to stay a member of the earthly realm, but I can't do it no more. So please, just entertain this humble soul for a few minutes of yer' time. I want the whole world to know about that damned Box, the one that could make you talk to the God Almighty and feel the Holy Spirit running through your veins.

"To save you the trouble of having to rummage through my wallet to find some identification, my name was Bill. Back in my prime though, I was better known as 'Raphael the Illuminating.' I took one of them fancy Italian names to carry around with me, 'cause most people wouldn't be caught up in the grandeur of 'Bill the Magician.' Since I was a young man, startin' when I was sixteen or seventeen, I'd been travellin' around with this group of performers who called themselves 'The Vargas Troubadour.' My momma left me in the orphanage right from when I was a little baby, and from what I could gather, my daddy died fightin' them Germans in the first World War. Some point down the line, they took me to see the Troubadour, and I did a cheesy little card trick for the head honcho that I learned from another boy there at the home. He liked it so much they took me right on the spot, and I was riding with 'em ever since. From the fancy suits and ties and skyscrapers up in New York down to the sun baked red clay of Macon, Georgia, we'd roll around in a big ol' Chevy semi that had 'PARADISE OR BUST!!!' painted bigger than shit on the side of it. We'd stop and do little and big cities both, wherever we thought we'd be able to make a dollar or two to keep us movin' along.

"I don't reckon that you could describe our little outfit as a 'sideshow' like some folk unaffectionately did throughout the years. We were a motley crew, to be sure, but our talents weren't just deformities and extra limbs like some of these other operations. There was me, of course, the obligatory magician. I didn't do no big tricks like flying or gettin' buried alive, but I had some decent slight-of-hand and card tricks that could get the crowd goin'. I even sawed a woman in half a few times, no kiddin'! We had Greta the Human-Bee, and her act was mostly just with balancing on them rings and flippin' around like a greased up monkey. Ferdy was our juggler, but he wasn't ever no good. He dropped more of them pins than he ever caught from what I seen. Wads the Clown was your standard bozo, but I think some of his material was a bit too high-brow for our audience, and for me too. He'd do a long routine where he'd just sit there and put on his make-up and slap on his nose, then people'd clap for that. I never understood it one bit. There was a few people who just helped with puttin' up and tearin' down our big ol' green Army canvas tent, but they didn't do any kind of performance. Every now and then, we'd pick up a new act on the road and they'd stay for however long was comfortable for them, then be back on their way again. Lil' Annie didn't do no show either, but she was just the sweetest little girl you could ever imagine. I reckon she was about fourteen years old, but I never did ask her. I don't even think she knew for sure. But she was like me; the troop picked her up from an orphanage and treated her real nice for a while. Then finally, we had the big man himself, Father Zoltan the Enlightened. He was our Ringmaster and 'Spiritual Advisor,' as he'd always say, but I always just called him Boss. That suited me just fine.

"All right, so we weren't no Ringling Brothers circus, and we didn't have enough money to get an elephant or tigers or any of that fluff. We just had one attraction that made us famous to the common rabble, something that would line the folks up from the city center out to our little set-up on the outskirts of town. The city folk were always more skeptical than the country boys, but they all left amazed the same. The official name of it, according to Father Zoltan, was 'The Grandiose Chamber of Electro-magnetic Communion with Our High and Mighty Lord the Almighty God.' That didn't roll off the tongue too well with anybody, so us performers, and the audiences that came, were just fine in callin' it 'The God Box.' At every stop during our tours, the God Box was the main event, and rumors spread far and wide about what this thing could do.

"The set-up for our performances was always the same. We'd make camp on a Thursday night. Father Zoltan would head out once we arrived and round up some local talent to help support the show. Mostly, he was searchin' for some strapping young lads to help us move around the heavier equipment and some fine lookin' young ladies to strut around and pass out fliers and coupons and such. He'd have the girls wear these real elegant, sequined get-ups that showed off some skin. He always called 'em 'Peacocks,' 'cause their whole purpose there was just to get folks lookin' at 'em and to stick around for a while.

All the day on Friday, we'd do some local advertisin', and set the agenda for what we'd be doin'. Then, Saturday and Sunday, we'd perform our acts. Everything always culminated towards the encore performance in the early evening; the unveiling of the God Box.

"Most of the show took place inside the tent, but the Box spectacle was always outside. Just lookin' at it from afar, it was none too impressive. Looked more like a phone booth than some fancy communicator with the Heavens, but I reckon it's what was inside that counted. Just a big, gray steel box with some expensive lookin' purple and red drapes hanging from the side, and a sliding door entrance that sealed ya in like a confessional booth. Once you went in, there'd be nothing but a little wooden stool in the corner and a big ol' picture of Jesus Christ starin' straight into your soul, judging you for all the sins you done committed the night before steppin' into that monstrosity. Father Zoltan would have all the crowd gather around, and give a big, important speech about how this was a once in a lifetime opportunity to speak directly to the Lord and Father Almighty, and how only two or three of them folks could experience it 'cause there just weren't enough hours in the day to get 'em all in. So he'd grab one or two volunteers from the audience (and these were legit patrons, not like some stooge I'd set-up before hand in one of my tricks!) and have 'em go into the God Box one at a time. Then, sure as the sun'd come up in the mornin', they'd come out lookin' pale and muttering nonsense for a few seconds before breathin' in some deep air and regaining their senses. Ain't a single one of them folks I ever seen come out of that Box and say that they didn't talk to the Lord, not one! And all their stories were different, but at the same time, just about the same. They all said they seen a big bright light, and they heard whispers and some of the Holy Word from the Bible and even some personal advice related to their lives!

"This thing was a real life miracle machine, and not one of them folks who went inside would say otherwise. They'd rant and rave and make a big ol' spectacle about it, and then there'd always be an uproar when Father Zoltan would tell the crowd that we couldn't put no more people in it for the night. He always told me, 'That's how ya keep 'em coming back. Gotta leave 'em wanting more.' But ya see, I never had no interest in personally goin' into that contraption myself. I wasn't no religious scholar, but I knew well enough that my Bible never said nothin' about boxes that could commune with Jesus the Lord and Savior, so I left good enough alone and never asked about it. I always had a funny feelin' about that thing though, from when I first started tourin' with the crew. Father Zoltan was real secretive about the God Box and never let any of the full-time performers go in it anyways. We couldn't even help with movin' it when it was time to hit the road again. It'd always be them local boys he'd hire on Thursday to hoist it up on the truck, and we kept our distance from it like he requested. I started to get a funny feelin' about it early on though, on account of seein' dead rats and critters surrounding the Box whenever it'd be time to leave. They hadn't been caught by no cat or fox neither. These little buggers looked like they died peacefully; not a single scratch or bite-mark on 'em. Every night after a performance, they circled around that magic box. I guess maybe it was a little morbid to go check on 'em like I did, but that's what got me thinkin' about the true nature of the chamber and start to think that maybe God didn't have nothin' to do with this after all.

"I reckon everything started to fall apart about six months ago. It was September of nineteen-forty-four, and the whole country was restless and wantin' to finish up the Great War goin' on in Europe as fast as possible. Me and Wads the Clown had a similar story. I ain't proud to say it, but we both pussy-footed out of servin' in the Army by fakin' injuries and dodgin' the draft as best we could. The way I looked at it, we was doing our part back at home, entertaining the folks waiting for their loved ones to get back and givin' 'em a little hope instead of just sittin' round and worrying. Tensions were growin' internally amongst us in the Vargas Troubadour, part from the declining number of people comin' out to see us, part from the lack of money we was gettin' from our shows, and part just being tired of doing the same old thing every night. I'd been on the road with 'em now for dang near fifteen years, and I didn't have a thing to show for it except for a fancy deck of playing cards with my name printed on 'em and a resume that could maybe get me a job washin' dishes for an old country buffet type restaurant.

"We'd stopped in Charleston for a regularly sched-uled performance, and I figured I'd go and talk to Father Zoltan to maybe get my head back on straight, or maybe quit the show altogether. I hadn't quite made up my mind about that at the time, but I thought maybe he could help me sort it all out. He'd always set up his office in one of the stand alone buildings nearby our camp site 'cause he always said he needed privacy before the performance began. Once we had settled in on the Thursday night like usual, I went up and knocked on his door and he called me in. I don't know if it bears mentionin', but that night he had this teenage boy there in his office with him. I can't remember his name right now for the life of me, but I think it was Anthony LaFoy or Anton LeCoy. Defi-nitely some kind of French soundin' surname. This kid was just leavin' as I got in there, but he had this look in his dark eyes as he passed me that made him look ten times his own age, like he had some deep understanding of the world that none of us other folk got. I didn't never see him again after he left Father Zoltan's office that night, but I remember it 'cause the Boss wasn't ever the same after that kid left. Zoltan told me that this kid was a member of another travelin' circus, and that he had some curious ideas about spirituality that were worth takin' note of. I thought that it was a little bit odd that he'd be listenin' to the advice of a boy about matters of the God Almighty, but Father Zoltan was always a strange fellow.

"So, I told him all about what I'd been thinkin', about how maybe I'd leave the Troubadour and try my hand elsewhere, or if maybe I could take on a more active role in the troop to keep myself from goin' stir crazy. I reckon I thought he'd take it bad and maybe throw me right out of his office, but he did just the opposite! Father Zoltan shot me a wry smile and shook his head, and I felt real comforted by that for some reason. He told me, 'Bill, yer one of our best acts and it'd be a dang shame to see you go. Why don't you come downtown with me tonight and find some help for the show, and maybe we can talk this out and get you thinkin' straight again?' Just with that, all of a sudden I felt recharged again, an' was real happy with the prospect of bein' involved. So, I told the Boss that I'd just go grab my jacket and we'd be on our way. He told me to pick up little Annie on my way back to take with us, and then we set off all together into the Charleston sunset.

"That whole time when we were walkin' around downtown, Annie held my hand real tight. I don't think she'd ever been in a city this big and full of life, but I remember she was makin' a real deliberate-like attempt to keep away from Father Zoltan as best she could. I didn't pay it no mind at the time though. As we'd pop in to little shops and bars here and there, the Boss would proposition any young lady that he thought was pretty enough to be a Peacock or a young man that looked like he could haul some heavy gear a ways and ask 'em to help out for the weekend. He offered a dollar a day, which ain't bad for just a little bit of walkin' and lifting, all things considered. We'd just about gotten all the folks we needed, and I started askin' some questions to the Boss that I'd always been curious about.

"'Mister Zoltan, where'd the God Box come from?' He told me that it was a family heirloom of his, but as best he knew, they originally found it somewhere in Africa and fit it with metal and some other fixin's throughout the years.

"'Mister Zoltan, does it really work? These people that go in there, they talk to our Father, no lie?' He just nodded and raised his eyebrows at me, with a little bit of a smirk formin' on his lips.

"'Mister Zoltan, is it true what some of them folks say? That afterwards, the people who go into the Box just disappear and never come back?' He stopped full-dead in his tracks after I asked that question, and did a real dramatic roll of his head towards me, bringin' his face real close to mine and grinning real wide. He stared me down for what seemed like a full ten minutes, and it felt like the whole world around us just came screechin' to a halt and was waitin' for an answer. I felt one single rain drop splash down on my nose, and I couldn't do nothin' but stare right back at him. 'Bill,' he told me, 'I want you to go into the the Grandiose Chamber of Electromagnetic Communion with Our High and Mighty Lord the Almighty God. You need to hear it for yourself, if you truly don't believe in its power.' He spoke real calm and collected. I breathed a deep sigh of relief, and I politely declined, fer' the reasons I said before. I had no interest in messin' with the established order, and that hadn't changed. Right after, he crouched down on one knee and leaned in close to lil' Annie and asked her if she wanted to try out the God Box. She just kept holdin' my hand even tighter than before and slid a little bit behind my leg, as if to hide from him and told him in a real timid voice, 'No thank you, sir.'

"Father Zoltan raised himself back up and shrugged, and said, 'Very well. I can respect that. But things will be changin' real soon in our little camp, and I want both of your support. I need to know that you believe in the Box, and that you believe in me.' I reckon I didn't have no reason not to, so I told him that I did, and Annie said she did too.

"We finished up the evenin' walkin' back to the campsite, but the mood was still a little bit tense. Father Zoltan was always real charismatic, and he even got me all riled up when he started talkin' about how that Adolf Hitler fella in Germany was killin' all the Jews and that he figured he might well be the Antichrist himself made manifest to end the world. I didn't know too much about the war except that they said it was worse than the first one, and it was bloody and full of heroes and villains and heartbreak and loss. Just as we were arrivin' back home, it started to drizzle just a little bit, and some big ol' rain clouds were rollin' in. Father Zoltan closed his eyes just outside of his office and stretched his arms all the way out at his sides, and looked up at the sky, seemin' like Jesus Christ Himself on the cross. He asked us, 'Do you feel it coming? You don't need the Box to communicate with the Lord, Bill, this is it, right now!' He breathed in real deep and then put his arm around me. 'Come to my office tomorrow night, at about eleven p.m after the performance,' he told me. 'That's when things will change, and I, alongside our Lord, will give you the direction that you need.' He kneeled down next to lil' Annie again and whispered somethin' in her ear that I couldn't quite make out, and then he was back in his office, callin' it quits for the night.

"That next morning, the rain hadn't let up, and it was keepin' a steady shower comin' down all day. Big ol' mud puddles were formin' up in the middle of camp site, and I didn't have nothin' to do except sit and watch as all the strong young men moved around bags and crates and the Peacocks walked back and forth lookin' for places to keep dry and for folks to give fliers to. I was perched up under an awning for one of the auxiliary buildings, and Wads the Clown was sittin' there too, just shootin' the shit with me. I think that Wads appreciated the ladies a bit too much, an' he'd always be makin' comments that I never fully appreciated about 'em when they'd walk by. This one lady, a Peacock in her full outfit strutted past, and made eye contact with us both as she went. I seen maybe she gave us a little wink, but it was probably just wishful thinkin'. She was a real pretty brunette, with a young lookin' face and some hips like you wouldn't be-lieve. She filled out that little uniform real nice, and you could tell she was proud of it. Wads leaned over close to me an' said, 'I'd like to ruffle her feathers up, ya know what I mean?' and he nudged me a few times and chuck-led. I reckon I did know, but I didn't say nothin' back. Then this redhead walked by, not a Peacock, but real gor-geous just the same, wearin' a low cut blouse that you could see under a bright yellow unbuttoned rain jacket. I think she was just there a little too early but I never did ask. Wads turned back to me again and said, 'I'd like to climb her like a tree and get up on the top, know what I mean?' and he started laughin' like there wasn't a thing funnier in the world. I didn't think much of that either, so I just chuckled for a second and paid him no mind. But then, I seen lil' Annie runnin' around and helpin' move some of the smaller stuff from the truck towards the tent.

She was all wet on account of the rain, and her clothes was stickin' to her body real close. Wads started elbowin' me in the ribs, and he looked at me and said, 'I'd like to crack her open like a coconut and drink the milk inside, you get me?' and then he was wigglin' his eyebrows real suggestive-like and grinnin'. Now, there was no denyin' that Annie was quite a looker. She was blonde and real fit, and was developin' pretty quick for her age, but I told Wads, 'Listen you sumabitch, that girl ain't but a teen, and you shouldn't be thinkin' that way about her. I don't wanna hear that kinda garbage 'bout her no more, ya hear?' He pouted like a boy who didn't get his way, and I decided it was time for me to go about my business and leave him be. I trotted out into the rain and helped Annie with what she was carryin', but when I got a close glance at her, she looked like she hadn't been to sleep in days. Real heavy and dark bags were circled round her eyes, and she looked like she could'a just collapsed and gone to sleep right there in the mud. I asked her if everything was okay, and she said yes and told me not to worry about it.

"The performance went on like usual that night. I did my act and got a nice standin' ovation. Wads was a bit more energetic than normal, and the folks appreciated that. Ferdy did some bad juggling, and Greta swung around on her rings under a big white spotlight. But just like always, the spectators started gatherin' around outside right around seven p.m, and the God Box was there on full display, ready to mystify and dazzle. Father Zoltan shushed the crowd, and they all listened to him rattle on and get real fiery and passionate about this opportunity to commune with the Lord God Almighty. It dawned on me that night that it'd been years since I'd really intently watched a full performance from Father Zoltan and his Box. I reckon it just became common place for me and I didn't pay it no mind, but tonight, I was watchin' with my full attention. I didn't know what the Boss wanted to show me after this was finished, an' I was a little bit nervous to tell the truth. So for tonight, I wanted to see exactly what happened.

"Father Zoltan finished up his speech to the crowd and asked for volunteers. The peoples' arms all shot up at the same time like bats outta hell, and they were all clamorin' to make themselves visible in hopes that they'd get picked over the rest. Zoltan perused the crowd with a careful eye, lookin' each prospect up and down. There was a crowd of about two-hundred or so folks trying to get in there, but like usual, he only picked three. The first pick was a common lookin' man from the city. He was probably in his mid-thirties, brown hair, plain clothes and a scruffy mustache. Zoltan walked through the crowd again, still considering and eyeballin' each hopeful that he passed by. He grabbed this other guy by the shoulders, and thrust him towards the front of the crowd. He was just about the same as the other man before him, just with no mustache. After a minute or two more of surveyin', Zoltan went all the way to the far side of the crowd and took the hand of that brunette Peacock me and Wads had seen struttin' about earlier, the one who Wads wanted to ruffle her feathers. He lifted up her hand like a true gentleman, gave it a little kiss and led her over to where the other two lucky men were standin' at.

"'Ladies and gentlemen,' he said to 'em all. 'These three fortunate souls will tonight act as a medium in the communication between our earthly realm and our Lord, the Alpha and Omega.' I'm paraphrasin' what Zoltan said, cause' I ain't no good with fancy speeches like he was, and I can't remember it all, but just know that the crowd was real curious to see the spectacle and started cheerin' and hollerin' for them to get put in the Box.

"I ain't never felt it before, but that night, I was anxious as all get-out before them people went in the chamber. Maybe I just got a weird feelin' from what Zoltan had told me about there bein' changes coming, or maybe I was still just confused about what to do with my life and I didn't even want to watch, like it woulda' been smarter for me just to walk away and never come back. But, I stayed there, and the show went on. Father Zoltan ran the show exactly the same as always. The rain had even let up just as everyone was gathering around the Box. That pretty Peacock girl went in there first, and the Boss went away to watch from the back of the audience. The whole crowd grew real silent after she entered, and it stayed that way for about five whole minutes. Not a word spoken between folks, just all eyes facing forward, waiting for some kind of response, like they were all waiting for the word of God themselves.

"At last, that metal door slid open, and the purple drape in front of it got pushed to the side as the Peacock girl came walkin' out. I had seen this a million times before; ain't nothing had changed. She was a little loopy, and started cryin' real big tears of joy and threw her arms up in the arm screamin', 'I heard it! I heard the voice of the Lord, praise be to Him!' As I was standin' there watchin', I felt Father Zoltan put his hand on my shoulder and he whispered to me, 'Go get her, and bring her back here to me.' I did like he asked, and worked my way up to where she was still shouting praises and actin' hysterical. I politely asked her to come with me, but she was too caught up in the moment to respond, so I just kinda gently took her hand and led her near the back to the Boss. She hugged him real tight then, and still cryin', started thankin' him for the opportunity and said that the Lord told her how she could better her life and exactly what His plan was for her. Mister Zoltan calmed her down a bit and told her to breathe real deep, and she did like he said.

He took her by the hand and said in a real cool voice, 'My lady. The Lord has truly blessed you. Please, return here tonight, at eleven, and come alone. I have heard the gospel. our God Almighty would like to speak with you again, if you would allow it.' She looked real excited at the idea, and Father Zoltan smiled and told her, 'Remember, come alone. Tell no one about your return.' She was bursting at the seams with what looked like pure joy, and she went skittering off back into the crowd. This was all familiar to me, except for askin' the folks to come back. I hadn't ever seen the Boss do that before, not once.

"Zoltan ran himself back up to the front of the crowd, and went through the same motions with the next guy. He gave his impassioned speech, and asked the guy with the mustache what his name was. He told everyone that it was Richie, and then he went on into the God Box. Five minutes later, same story. He came out, overwhelmed by the Voice, and said he seen visions of the end of times and how it was comin' soon, but he seemed real pleased with it just the same and said it was beautiful. The Boss told me to do the same thing for him that I did with the Peacock lady and bring Richie to the back, and I did. Zoltan gave him the same invitation, said for him to come on back at eleven, all by himself. Then, as you can imagine, the same thing happened with the third man, who said his name was Grady. He went in the Box, he came out shoutin' the Gospel, and Zoltan told him to come back alone at eleven. That was it for the show. The crowd made a desperate plea for some more folks to be able to try out the Box, but Father Zoltan just told 'em we'd be back through Charleston again someday and they'd maybe get their shot if they returned. We already told 'em that the Sunday show was gonna be cancelled on account of the rain, so they'd just have to wait it out. By nine p.m., just about the whole crowd had gone about their way, and the camp was deserted and dark like as if no one had ever even set foot there.

"I'd sat with Annie for the next two hours or so near-by Zoltan's office, waitin' for Richie, Grady and the Pea-cock lady to come back. I remember I couldn't stop my foot from tappin' on the ground. Me and Annie didn't say nothin' to each other, 'cause we was nervous just the same. Then finally, this shadow came creepin' out of the darkness from off in the distance, and as they made their way a bit closer I saw that it was Richie. Not too long lat-er, Grady and the Peacock showed up too, and it seemed like everything was ready to go.

"Father Zoltan came out of his office real casual like, and greeted 'em all standing out in the mud. The God Box was still set-up where it was before, and I seen two or three of them dead rats around it already. Our three guests were chit-chatting amongst themselves, and then Wads the Clown showed up too, wearin' some kind of black rain jacket with a hood that I ain't never seen him in before. He looked real serious though, and didn't say nothin'.

"'Ladies and gentlemen,' Zoltan told 'em, 'Tonight we stand on the boundary between salvation and damna-tion.' He looked real pleased with himself, and was talkin' and leadin' us all over to the Box as he spoke. 'You felt today that this miracle is real, that you truly can speak to the Lord. But to embrace our God, you must pass the test.' When he said that, all three of them folks looked a little worried and started glancin' back and forth at each other. Zoltan told 'em they had one last chance to leave if they didn't want to be a part of the trial, and Richie asked him, 'What kind of test exactly is this, sir?' Zoltan told him, 'A test of faith. Believe in me, and believe in the word of the Lord and you shall be rewarded.' I guess Richie didn't be-lieve, 'cause he kind of chuckled and apologized and said he maybe made a mistake and then he slinked off into the night away from the camp. Smart kid, that Richie. But Grady and the Peacock was still there, ready to try out their dedication to the Gospel.

"Then Father Zoltan explained to 'em the rules. No peekin', no listenin' and no talkin' to the person before you. It was all about the faith, he said. So, Grady said that he'd go first, and then Wads escorted the lovely young Peacock about a hundred feet back and asked her to go down to her knees. He pulled out a kind of burlap sack and jammed it on over her head real quick, then strapped it down at the neck pretty tight from what I seen. Up at the Box, Zoltan slid open the door and motioned for Grady to step on in. He pulled the entrance closed, and then he walked up and stood beside me and Annie. 'Bill,' he told me, 'I'm glad that you can finally be a part of this. We're all a family here. You too, Annie.' I looked down at Annie, and she looked back up at me, fear in her precious little eyes. 'Okay, Mister Zoltan,' I told him. 'I believe in you like I done said before.'

"We stood there for about ten minutes, and then I heard some grunting and groaning comin' from inside the box. It sounded like someone was hurt, and I started to run up there but Zoltan stopped me. He said 'No. This is the test. He must exit on his own,' and I stayed back. 'Bout five minutes later, the door came slidin' open, real slow. I couldn't see it too clear on account of the night, but what came out of that Box wasn't the same man who went in. He kinda limped outta there with a hand up on his face, and was movin' real slow towards us all. Zoltan slowly approached, and I followed up with Annie in tow. When we got closer, I got a good look at Grady's face. Streaks of red ran down it like some sort of injun warrior, and his hands and clothes were stained, dark red splattered on a white shirt. I told Annie to run along and go back to her room and not come back, and she did like I said. Zoltan was still keepin' his distance from this husk, and said to him, 'Grady. Grady! How do you feel?' I thought that was a downright dumb question. This man had blood all over him, and he clearly wasn't in no right state of mind! But Grady looked up at him, with a calm gaze in his eyes, and told him, 'I'm fine, sir. Just fine.' Zoltan smiled, patted him on the back, then told him to go over to his office and Grady done like he said. As Grady walked by, I seen a little bit of what happened. He had some big ol' gash marks on one of his arms and a smaller one on his face, like someone had peeled him up like an apple. I was real panicked, and I asked Zoltan what was goin' on. He said, 'Bill, he passed the test. This is a joyous day. Now for the encore.' Wads the Clown came up out of the shadows again and pulled the Peacock off of her knees and took the bag off her head. I guess she heard a little bit of what happened, cause' she changed her mind real quick about wanting to go in that Box! She tried and pleaded and said to Zoltan, 'Please sir, I had a change of heart, and I ain't interested no more in this little freak show of yours!' But Wads had a good grip on her arm and they weren't havin' any of it. 'It's too late, my dear. The Lord has chosen you! You must take the test.' She was pleadin' and cryin' as they forced her towards that open door, and gosh darnit, this is where I could have stopped it all. But I didn't. It ain't right that I didn't do nothin' to stop 'em, but I can't change the fact that I didn't.

"She put up a fight all the way into the Box, and I think Wads even slammed the door on her hand as she was trying to claw her way out. Zoltan slapped a padlock on the outside of that thing, and we could all hear her sobbin' and beggin' for a minute or two. Zoltan told Wads to go check on Grady, which he did, and I just stood there listenin' and beatin' myself up on the inside. But I didn't have to wait for long. She got real quiet all of the sudden, and then we just stood there in silence.

"Five minutes passed by. Then ten. Zoltan put his hand on his chin, and made a real obvious sigh like he wasn't too happy. I didn't have any words to say to him then. Finally, he said, 'She has failed. Stay here, Bill.' He walked on up to the door and unlocked it, and slid it real casually out of the way. I saw he looked down for a minute, then he bent over and started dragging that poor girl towards me. I just waited right where I was at, too scared and weak to do a damn thing. This poor Peacock was just gettin' dragged through the mud like her body was a used couch gettin' ready to be put in the Dumpster, and when Zoltan got to me, he just dropped her arms and she collapsed into a puddle at my feet.

"Now, I couldn't see real clear still because of the dark, but I coulda sworn that girl was dead when he was draggin' her. I didn't move a muscle in my body, 'cause I didn't know what to think at all. Zoltan told me to kneel down and look at her, and after a moment of internal debatin', I did it. But ya see, this Peacock wasn't dead after all! She was still breathin' and her eyes were half open, but she was in real bad shape. She seemed like she was tryin' to say something, but just some blood and spit was comin' out of her mouth every time she'd open it. Almost reminded me of a fish after you got it out of the lake, just gaspin' for air in a bucket.

"Zoltan told me, 'Bill, this is what failure looks like. She was a harlot, and the Lord Almighty had no useful plan for her. She wasted this opportunity. Now kill her.' I was shocked just like you could imagine, and I jumped up and told ol' Mister Z that he done lost his mind! But he was just as cool as ever, and he shook his head and said, 'Bill, you ain't no ordinary man now. You're part of this family. You're involved. Even if you run, you have your hands in this now, and you can never get away. Join me, join the family, and follow us to salvation.'

"Now, this is why I said at the start that I can't never make up for what I done. 'Cause after that, I still felt guilty, but my need for bein' a part of that group overpowered my sense of decency and right an' wrong. So I did it, just like Mister Zoltan said, with Wads the Clown standin' in the back watchin' and grinnin'. I kneeled back down next to that gaspin' Peacock, and I slid the knife that Wads gave me right into her soft belly. I was scared, so I just kept pushin', and got it all the way in so deep that I could feel my hand up to my knuckles get warm from her insides. She didn't have much of a fight left in her, and she just stopped breathin'. This was a beautiful lady just twenty minutes ago, and now she's layin' there dead in the mud on account of me and the Box.

"Then just silence. I didn't want nothin' to do with nobody then, but I sure as hell didn't want to have time to think about what I just done. So I asked Mister Zoltan what needed to happen, and he said that me and Wads would take the Peacock and give her a 'proper burial,' in his words.

"We rolled the Peacock up real haphazardly into an old carpet about an hour after I killed her, and threw her into the back of the pick-up that Zoltan said he borrowed from a friend. Wads was drivin', and it took us about an hour or so to get deep enough into the woods so that nobody would be watchin'. There wasn't a lot said durin' that ride, but Wads didn't seem bothered one bit. He was just whistlin', and even singing along to some of them catchy tunes that came up on the radio. We found a nice little clearing down by a riverbed about twenty miles outside of town, and then we dragged the carpet off the truck and set it down in the grass. I'd been thinkin' long and hard that whole trip, and somehow I justified it to myself, sayin' that maybe the Box was real, and we really were special, and that Father Zoltan had a plan for all of this. He saved me from the orphanage; he could save me now. That was my logic.

"The carpet was heavier than I thought, but it wasn't too much trouble fer' me and Wads to get it out pretty far into the woods. Then we started diggin'. All night long, it seemed to me, but we both done an equal portion of the work. We talked while we worked, and Wads said he used to be a grave digger before he joined the Vargas Troubadour, and I believed him I suppose. But we didn't say nothin' 'bout killin' her, or about the Box. We wrapped it up when Wads said it was good enough, and we unrolled that poor girl from her fabric coffin. I can still remember her face, and she looked so peaceful, like nothin' in the world was wrong. A little discolored, but other than that like a little angel, and I remember thinkin' that it was a pretty profound moment for me. Then Wads chimed in and said real sudden, 'Bill. I still wanna ruffle her feathers.' I felt sick all of a sudden, and I didn't say nothin'. I just walked on back to the truck and got in, hopin' that the clown would be right behind me and we'd just get on back to the camp. 'Bout fifteen minutes later, Wads came strollin' up, whistlin' again, and started the engine. We didn't say nothin' more to each other that night.

"After that evening, everything looked different to me. I don't know if Ferdy or Greta knew about the killin', but they went about their lives like normal. Lil' Annie asked me what happened, but I told her that it was nothin' and that she shouldn't worry about it none. She didn't believe me, but she was smart enough to just leave well enough alone. Grady stuck around, though. He passed his test in the Box, but he was just like a zombie walkin' around the camp and helpin' with whatever Mister Zoltan told him. He didn't say nothin' to anybody, even when they asked him, and he always looked like he was just ready to keel over at a moment's notice. I started spendin' all my time with Annie, whenever I could. We got real close over them next few days, and she even told me that she sometimes wanted to run away because she didn't like Zoltan one bit. I told her that this was her family now, and if she don't like him, at least she had me to look out for her. I felt real good about that, and just about the only peace I got was from helpin' sweet little Annie throughout the day.

"The show moved on like it always had, except at every stop now I was involved in the God Box spectacle just like the first time, and we cut the number of shows per week down to just one on Saturday night. People kept comin' to see it, and once a week we'd go through the motions. Zoltan would choose the volunteers, they'd get invited back, and then we'd have that same ceremony with me and Wads. The results were 'round about the same every time. Mister Z would choose his people, normally two men and one Peacock, and when they returned on their promises of 'enlightenment,' they'd get back in that Box. I seen all kinds of crazy shit durin' this little stretch. One guy damn near cut his entire hand off before he came out, but he passed the test. Some girl down south in Pensacola somehow managed to cut her entire stomach open and spill her guts out all over the place before we could even open the door; she didn't pass, but cleanin' it up after was a nightmare. I found out later that there was always some kinda ceremonial knife in there before people would go in; that's how they'd all end up disfigured in some way or another. They'd be inflicting the wounds on themselves, an' the survivors would say that God made 'em do it. Me and Wads would always take the failures out into the wilderness and dump 'em, just like the first time.

"After about two months or so of this, we'd rounded

up quite the collection of people who passed the test, round about twenty, and they all stuck around. We even had to buy a new semi just to accommodate 'em all! Every one of em' were like Grady after the test, though. Quiet, bags under their eyes, normally bandaged up on account of the wounds they'd given themselves. Mopin' around like they didn't have a single thought in their heads, just slavin' away on whatever project Mister Zoltan gave 'em to do. I didn't like havin' these folks around. They were scarin' little Annie, and I didn't know what purpose they was servin' by hanging around so long. I reckoned I was in this mess deep enough now that I could talk to Father Zoltan about it, so I went an' knocked on his door one day when we were in Mobile, Alabama to get some answers.

"I was about to knock, but I heard somethin' from standing outside. I put my ear up on the door real stealthy-like, and I heard this little panting and what sounded like cryin'. The sounds of someone being erotic, but not likin' it none too much. I figured that Zoltan had one of them Peacocks in there with him, as he was apt to do, so I just sat down and waited. But after about ten minutes, the door came openin' up and out walked little Annie with tears in her eyes! She looked over at me real embarrassed like, and went runnin' off without sayin' a word. Boy, I tell you what! I was fumin' mad, and went stormin' into Zoltan's office like a bull in a china shop! Just as I was raging in there, he was still buttonin' up his pants, lookin' real pleased with himself. I grabbed that shyster by his collar and slammed him up against the wall, and yelled at him, 'You sumabitch! I know you ain't no good to all them common folks, but why'd you gotta ruin Annie like that?' And just like he always was, Zoltan just calmly stared me down and said, 'Hey, Bill. Put me down.' He wasn't the type to get real emotional about things, and I figured it'd be best to try and reason with him rather than get violent. So I done like he asked, and he walked over to his desk and offered me a drink of bourbon. I said okay and sat down.

"'Mister Zoltan', I told him, 'I don't care none what you do with anybody else. But you leave that little girl alone, or else me and you have got big problems. She's just about the only thing I care about in this world, and I'll do what I gotta do to protect her.' He reassured me that everything was completely consensual, but that if it'd make me happy, he wouldn't diddle around with her no more. I didn't believe him one bit, but there wasn't much I could do apart from just say 'okay' and keep an eye on the situation.

"I reckon I'd forgotten why I went there in the first place, but Mister Zoltan reminded me and asked, 'What can I help you with today, Bill?' Then I remembered and went right into it. I asked him why we had all these folks comin' along with us, and why they didn't say nothin' and why they did exactly what Zoltan told 'em to do without question. He took a sip of his drink and asked, 'What do you know about Judas, Bill?' I told him that I didn't want to get off-topic, and that I needed some answers, but he just repeated his question again. So I told him what I knew. That Judas was a traitor and that he betrayed our Holy Father, Jesus Christ, and that I hoped that devil traitor was burnin' in Hell for the rest of eternity. But Zoltan shook his head real slow, and said, 'That's what most people think, but what about looking at it from a different perspective?' I didn't know what that rascal was talkin' about. I learned in church that it was real cut an' dry; that Judas fella was a bad guy, bottom line. He continued on and said, 'Think about it like this, Bill. Do you believe that we have free will, or does God have a plan for us all, and we're predestined to live that life?' I told him that I thought there was a plan for everything. 'So then, was God's plan for Judas not to betray Jesus? Was Judas not blessed from the start to have such an intimate role in the gospel? How could one blame Judas for his act if it was already planned beforehand?' I hadn't never thought about it like that, and I figure it made a little bit of sense. He kept on talkin' though. 'And what of free will? Was it not necessary for Jesus to die on the cross so that we might all be absolved of our sins? What if Judas intentionally chose to martyr himself for humanity so that we might all be saved? Didn't someone have to do it?' I hadn't never thought of that either, but I was startin' to get frustrated because I didn't go in there for no philosophical babble. I wanted to know about these folks who went in the Box.

"I sipped my drink that he gave me for the first time during our conversation, and I thought it tasted a little funny, but I wasn't ever a big bourbon drinker so I didn't know it was off. 'Mister Zoltan, why are you keeping these folks around who go in the God Box, and why are some of 'em dying when they go in there?' He set his drink down on the desk and leaned forward at me, motioning with his finger for me to come in closer and I did. 'I'm building an army, Bill. An army of the Lord.' He said it with a real raspy whisper, like he was tellin' a secret that no one else in the world could know. I asked him what for, 'cause it didn't make no sense for a travelin' show to need a militia. He said, 'The very nature of the world is changing. I know that you don't believe in the Box, I've seen it in your eyes. But I have talked to our God Almighty, and he showed me what I must do. Adolf Hitler is the devil incarnate, Bill. He's fulfilling all the prophecies, and he's killin' all them Jews over in Europe.' I started feelin' a little woozy right about at this point, but I kept on listenin' like I ain't never heard nothin' more interesting in my life. 'I will be this generation's Judas. I have volunteered my body to do the Lord's work, no matter the cost. I will sacrifice everything that I know is good and righteous and be seen as a villain to all so that I can save our people. But, to do this, I need an army to fight the devil from Germany. He will come here, eventually, and I will be ready for him.' Every word that this madman was sayin' now was ringing in my head. The room was circlin' around and I started seein' these real bright spots in the corners of my eyes. I kept tryin' to listen to him, but every word just kept getting' further and further apart. The last thing I heard him sayin' there was, 'I'm sorry, Bill. You are not a part of the Lord's plan anymore.' Then it was just all black.

"I don't know how long I was out for, but I can't imagine it was too terribly long. I woke up in a big ol' puddle of mud and feelin' like a sack of shit. My whole body below the neck was paralyzed, and all I could do was lay there and look around. I figured out that I was behind Mister Zoltan's office, 'cause I could see the God Box off in the distance from around the corner of the building where my head was. It was a Thursday night an' we had just set up camp earlier in the day. When I originally went into the office the sun was up, but it was pretty dang dark now, just light enough to make out some shapes. But, somethin' was different, apart from the sudden bout of paralysis. I could smell this real rotten stench flowin' through my nostrils, and the longer I layed there, I started seein' more and more of them colors flashing in the corners of my eyes. I asked myself all kinds of questions then, like, 'Is this how I'm gonna die?' and, 'What the hell did I ever go along with all this for, anyways?' Everything was spinnin', and havin' this regret in me wasn't helpin' none. So I just stayed there, and in that moment, I remember resignin' myself to the Lord and askin' him to send me to Hell or whatever other plan he done made for me. I thought that was gonna happen too, and I was real peaceful. Nothin' but the sound of the crickets chirpin' in the night and this feeling of calm that kept pulsin' through me, over and over again. And just when I thought I could feel the embrace of our God, somethin' rustled me up good.

"Out there in the distance, over near the God Box, I heard a little scream and I knew right away that it was Annie. I couldn't see nothin' too well on account of the darkness and these spots all over the place, but I knew it was her voice, and it sounded like she was strugglin'. It was tough to make out, but I could hear ol' Zoltan and Wads too, just barely, and I heard 'em laughin' and sayin' that she was gonna go in the Box and join the army proper. Well, I just wasn't havin' none of that, so I mustered up all the strength I could and started to push myself up outta that mud and onto my feet. I was just movin' inches at a time, but I done it. First onto a knee, then all the way up on two feet. I don't remember how long it took me, but just as I was gettin' ready to move, I seen Wads lock the box with that ol' padlock, and Zoltan was already gone and outta sight. I took one step forward to go an' get her, but then I walked straight into the mouth of Hell itself.

"I know it sounds absurd, but with every step I took towards that Box, I was descending deeper into the flames! I guess it's hard to explain, but I took one step forward and I seen fire shoot up all around me formin' a corridor right towards where Annie was at. Then the next step, and I seen all manner of demons and devil's and foul creatures I don't even wanna think about start peekin' their heads from outta the ground. Another step and I could hear Annie's voice amplified a thousand times in my head, screamin' for me to help her and that she was dyin'. The next step and I started hearin' other people talkin' from outta thin air and tellin' me that the devil from Germany was on his way here. But I kept walkin' right through that. I was pissin' my pants in fear, but I just knew I had to get Annie out of that Box. I didn't see Wads anywhere, on account of all the fire and brimstone in my peripherals, but I didn't let that bother me none. It felt like a twenty mile hike to get what was probly' a hundred feet, but I made it, and I grabbed a big ol' rock sittin' nearby and smashed and hit that padlock until it came fallin' off.

"Soon as I opened the door, Annie came fallin' right out, lookin' dead as a doornail. And Lord o' Lord, did I cry my eyes out! Didn't take but a few seconds for me to start bawlin' like a baby, 'cause I knew this was all my fault. Them demons I was seein' were still there, huddled around and just watchin' as I cradled this little girl in my arms. Starin' down at her, she looked like a little angel with a holy white glow around her, just calm and tranquil as could be. It almost reminded me of that first night with that Peacock, and I felt the same kind of remorse. I picked her up, and started walkin' away from the Box, not knowin' what I was gonna do next. But then she opened her eyes, just a little bit! She started quiverin' at the lip like she wanted to say somethin' and, after a little bit of effort, she opened her mouth. She just said one word, 'Vengeance.' But it wasn't her voice that I heard. It was somethin' deep and just spittin' of evil. I didn't mind that none, though; she was right. I set her down in the grass and all of a sudden I felt a new strength come through me, somethin' dark and powerful that I ain't never felt before. I started stompin' towards Zoltan's office with a cravin' for revenge like the world ain't never gonna see again. I told myself right then, 'This man will die by my hand, tonight.'

"All the flames and monsters I'd been seein' were gone now, but I still had a mean tunnel vision that pointed me straight towards where Zoltan and Wads were at. Just as

I was about to reach the building, Wads popped up outta nowhere and grabbed me around the neck. I dispatched him real quick and flipped him over my shoulder, slammin' his dumb clown ass to the ground. He started babblin' some type of apology soon as he saw the murderous look in my eye, but I didn't give him no chance, 'cause the damage had already been done. I took my heel and put it straight through his jaw, meetin' the pavement underneath with the heel of my boot. I looked down and didn't see nothin' but a pool of dark red blood and some white make-up smeared on the side of my footwear. Wads the Clown was gone. Told his last joke, I reckon. One more to go.

"I paused for a moment outside of Zoltan's door, 'cause I figured it'd be best if I got the jump on him. I took a deep breath then rammed my shoulder into the door, bustin' it open. But, that sumabitch wasn't in there! I was about to turn right back around again an' continue the hunt, but I seen somethin' on his desk that caught my attention. The whole room smelt like that awful stuff from when I was layin' in the mud, and it seemed to be comin' from a little tank right there in the corner of the office. I started toolin' around some, and I seen all kinds of notes that mentioned 'hydrogen cyanide' and all other manner of chemicals. Some of 'em I was familiar with as pesticides, but the others I ain't never seen before. There was a little tube attached to it, and I started followin' it down the wall. It went down a small hole in the corner of the buildin', and straight into the ground, running straight towards the Box. I reckon just as I started putting it all together in my head, Zoltan smashed me from behind with somethin' heavy, and I went tumblin' to the floor. He jumped on top of me and started chokin' me with both hands.

"'Bill', he was sayin', 'You're supposed to be dead.' I

looked back up at him and told him, 'But I ain't, sir.' And he kinda laughed at that for a minute, but then kept on stranglin' me. I was startin' to feel woozy again like before, so I didn't have no strength left in me to fight back all that well, but I done my best. He started tellin' me, 'These chemicals are not why people have experiences with the Lord when they go in the Box. They simply assist the process!' He seemed real defensive about me seein' all that stuff, but he didn't get a chance to finish. Just as he seemed like he was about to tell me his whole elaborate plan, he went flyin' off of me to the side and a big ol' splash of his blood came droppin' down on my face.

"I seen Annie standin' there behind where Zoltan used to be at, and she didn't say nothin'. She just walked straight over to where that bastard was layin' on the ground and started stabbin' him until he wasn't takin' no more breaths. Then she stabbed him again, and again. I reckon she plunged that knife into him 'bout forty or fifty times. After she was done she just dropped that knife there on his body and walked out of the room. No fancy monologue from Mister Zoltan, no clever words. Just him facin' his own mortality. I figure he's in Hell right now, alongside ol' Wads the Clown, eyeballin' some other girls that might be down there too and makin' inappropriate comments about 'em. But I ain't one to judge nobody, not considerin' what I done myself.

"I followed Annie out there into the foggy night, and we had a conversation and I told her what she needed to do to get away from here and how I couldn't go along with her. She cried some with me, and she begged me to go too, but I told her that this was how things needed to be, and it'd be best fer' her just to get along and try to live a normal life. I tried to pass on everything in those few minutes that I learned from my time on the road, and then she walked off into the moonlight, lookin' back one or two times before disappearin' into the horizon.

"Sorry if that was a little long winded, but I reckoned it'd be best if ya'll could make sense of all the murders and missin' folks along the East coast over these last few months. And before you go tryin', don't bother to try and find little Annie; that ain't even her real name. I told her how to lay low and just put all of this behind her. She's a smart girl, and she don't need this chapter in her life ever comin' back up again. So, that's it then. I still hear them voices inside my head from when I was pullin' her out of the Box, and they're still tellin' me to do just what Zoltan was doin'–to build an army, and to fight the devil. But that ain't right, so I'm just gonna end this before I end up like him.

"'Our Father, hallowed be yer' name, through kingdom come, yer' will be done, on Earth as it is in Heaven. Give us this day, our daily bread, and forgive us our trespasses as we forgive those who trespassed again You; lead us not to temptation, but deliver us from evil; through the power and the glory, Amen.' That was always one of my favorites. Goodbye, ya'll."

PENSACOLA MERMAID TANK

AMELIA MANGAN

I collected Jenny Hanivers.

They sell them at carnivals, at night. Other places and other times too, I suppose, but I only ever saw them at carnivals, and I only ever saw carnivals at night.

They pass them off as dead mermaids. The Jenny Hanivers, I mean. But they're not. Of course, they're not. They're manta rays, dead and dried out and painted. Their bodies all cut up. Pieces sliced off them until they look halfway human. Their eyes are frozen and crinkled and black, and their mouths gape in dead rictus, skull-smiles.

Every time I bought one, every time my money slipped away in some methed-out carny's greasy paw, I went back to whatever hotel I was staying in at the time, took one of my jars from the trunk of my rental and went back to my room, hoping no one would see me. I'd place the Jenny Haniver inside the jar and fill it up with tap water. Then I'd take one of the packets of salt from my pocket – a packet with a label on it that read New York or

Baltimore or Anaheim or Tampa – and I'd tip the whole thing into the water, watching the white crystals blossom and swirl and melt and fade. I carried labels with me, too; cheap, glue-backed things, the kind you'd see on the front of a kid's notebook, with flowers and cartoons and NAME and AGE and CLASS. I licked the backs, feeling my tongue go numb, and slapped them onto the jars. Under NAME I wrote my own. Sometimes I thought I should try to come up with names for the Jenny Hanivers, but what would be the point? All of them were named "Jenny Haniver." That was all the name they'd ever have. All the name they'd ever need.

When I was done, I'd take the jar back down to the car. Didn't matter what time it was; it had to be done straight away. I'd lock it away in the trunk with all the others. I had about four dozen Jennies now and the trunk was getting crowded. Starting to smell like salt water and brine. I didn't mind. I kind of liked it. Sometimes I'd lean closer and inhale, so deep I could taste the salt at the back of my throat.

It made my limbs tingle. The whole exercise. The whole ritual. A tingling like tiny feet running all up and down my neck and my arms and my legs. Especially my legs. I felt it when I was driving, felt it when I checked into a hotel, felt it when I was bottling the Jennies, and felt it, especially, at the carnivals. On the hunt.

I only lived at carnivals. I must have once had a job, family, friends–people. But I only remembered carnivals – sickly pink cotton-candy sugar and gritty hot-dog mince, screaming kids and sawdust, wet straw and bright lights, rickety roller-coasters and chipped-paint carousels, unscary ghost trains and inaccurate fortune-tellers and dead-eyed carnies and the sideshows, where you never quite got what you wanted or wanted what you got.

Carnivals. In every state, in every city. Every time I arrived someplace new I scanned the papers for carnival ads, announcements, articles. Some carnivals I followed from place to place. I became so obsessed with one particular carnival that they finally banned me.

I wandered endless boardwalks, felt an eternity of planks riding up and down beneath my feet. The best ones were by the sea. The music and the cries sank down into the waves, shaded away to silence. By the sea, I felt close to something, close to an understanding, that understanding I searched carnival after carnival to find. But it never truly came. I lived my life, instead, as a sleepwalker, an insomniac; haunted by a dream I could never quite recall.

The carnival in Pensacola was different. I had to give it that. A tiny ad, right down at the very bottom of the last page of the classifieds, in a free weekly entertainment guide so cheap the print shucked off onto your fingers if your hand even hovered over the page. Its pitch was simple:

MERMAID CARNIVAL
This Sunday
Deep in the Heart of the Swamp
Down Past Johnson's Gator Farm
* COME ONE COME ALL *

I wondered if maybe it was some kind of scam, to get suckers out in the boondocks and rob them.

Even as I wondered, I knew I'd go.

I had to take a boat. A rusty old scow. Only three

other passengers, two of them with hats pulled down low and cigarette-drooping mouths. The carny drove us in silence. The water was still; the birds were silent. It was beginning to get dark.

The carny dropped us off at a makeshift dock with white-painted planks. A cardboard sign tacked to a post: THIS WAY TO MERMAID CARNIVAL. A wobbly arrow beckoned us on.

We trooped down the pier onto the wet mushy bank, into the trees. Spanish moss and limp black branches and tangled white roots. Thick wet fog, greasy on the skin. Sharp taste at the back of the throat – rotting plants and gasoline. Mosquitoes bit. Wings rustled. Dark things splashed quietly, and I thought of the gator farm.

Lights ahead. Thin, murky. Long strings of fairy lights, scattered through the trees. Strung up over a long wooden boardwalk, overlooking the water. A new boardwalk. Only just set up. I could smell the fresh-cut wooden planks, the tacky paint. In this tiny, cramped little space, there were booths, crammed shoulder-to-shoulder; rides, broke-down and rusted and old. Victorian-old, antique-old. Food stands filled with nothing you'd want to eat. Silent carnies in ragged clothes. A speaker, hooked up haphazardly to a post. Crackling tunes echoed through the swamp, burlesquing merriment.

Full dark now, and the next boat didn't leave for an hour. Maybe they'd at least have some Jennies for sale. I stepped right up.

There were others there. Only a handful. They looked disappointed, resentful. Some were heading back to the dock. I resolved to go with them as soon as the hour was up. I didn't.

I ate the cotton candy. Rode the carousel. Tried to win a teddy bear. Lost money, lost time. Two hours passed and I never knew where they went. All the while, I asked every carny I met where I might find a Jenny Haniver. Mostly, I got shrugs and grunts.

The night was deep now. I was thinking, finally, about going back. That's when I saw him. He must've been there the whole time, but I never saw him until I'd just about decided to give up on the whole thing.

He was a carny; had to be. Finely dressed, though. No rags, no tattoos. Tailored vest, silk shirt, watch-chain. Porkpie hat angled just so. I couldn't tell if he was young or old, but he leaned against a signpost, his back against the wood, blocking out the words, as if he owned the place. Maybe he did.

I approached and he just watched. Not saying anything. No megaphone, no sales pitch.

"Hi," I said.

"Howdy," he said.

"Do you work here?"

"I surely do."

"What do you do?"

"Barker."

"You're not barking."

"People hear me clear enough."

"Can you help me?"

"Hope so."

"Do you know where I might find a Jenny Haniver? You know, to buy?"

"A Jenny Haniver."

"Yes. You know, those manta rays–"

"I know Jenny Hanivers. Them fake mermaids. Them dead, dried-up, fake mermaids."

"Yeah."

"We don't got no fake mermaids."

"Oh. All right –"

I turned.

"We got a real one."

I turned back.

He pushed off from the sign and its words became clear:

MERMAID TANK.
SEE HER.

A tent behind the sign. Thick purple silk. Securely closed.

"How much?" I asked.

The air was hot inside. Close. My sweat clung to me, leaked through my clothes. The smell of incense and brine, one wound around the other.

No lights, no adornment. Nothing in the tent. Nothing but the tank.

Made of glass and only as long and as wide as a human body. A glass coffin. Right out of a fairy tale. Aqua light shimmered from inside it, threw swirls and ripples across the dark silk, across the carny's pale skin, into my tired eyes.

The coffin was full of water, bubbling and hot. Steam rose, stinking of salt. Black seaweed shivered and waved and parted and, underneath, there she was. There she lay.

Her eyes were closed and her chest didn't move. She was sleeping, or unconscious, or dead. I didn't much care which. Her eyelids were white pearls. Her hair colorless wrackweed. Arms folded over her chest, and the arms shaped down to shoulders, and the shoulders down to breasts and hips down to glimmering white scales and scales down to a long, ragged fin. Some of her scales were flaking off. Someone had painted her fingernails; the paint was blue and chipped.

"She's dead," I said to the carny.

"Ain't," said the carny. "Just sleeping. Only ever sleeping."

I leaned down over the tank. The only barrier between us was water.

"Do people touch her?" I asked.

The carny shrugged.

"Can I touch her?" I asked.

The carny shrugged.

I wiped my palm on my shirt and leaned closer. My fingertips skimmed the water.

Her eyes opened.

I saw myself. My own face. Leaning over me from beneath a curtain of water. The back of my head touched glass. I breathed water. My face undulated above me, blurred, distorted and featureless.

I pulled back so fast I splashed myself. My heart damn near burst.

"What the hell is she?" I asked the carny. My words came out so fast they slurred. "What did I just see?"

The carny looked back at me. His eyes steady, almost as empty as hers.

"You saw," he said, "whatever you had to see."

I made it out of the swamp. Don't recall doing it. Got back to my hotel and I don't recall doing that either.

I slept. I woke. I slept again.

I walked around in the daytime, walked around at night. I ate at diners. I pocketed salt. I ate the salt. I drank the salt. I was never thirsty, not ever. I never had been, and I'd never wondered why.

I looked in bathroom mirrors and tried to find myself. All I saw was water. Water and faces peering back at me. Faceless faces. Devoid of feeling and meaning.

My whole life had been searching. Searching, and collecting. Jenny Hanivers. Little falsehoods, little lies. Little shadows of the real. I had searched.

I had searched too far.

I had found.

I woke up one night and my legs were gone. Where they had been, they tingled.

I woke up again and my legs were back.

I woke up again and my legs were not legs but a long stretch of scales terminating in a single ragged fin.

I woke up and woke up and woke up and never, never truly came awake.

I knew now what I had seen, what I had had to see. That my life, my whole life, had been no more than a dream, the dream of a sleeping mermaid in a tank in a tent in the middle of a Pensacola swamp out past where the gators wait.

The tingling in my limbs grew stronger and stronger and would not be ignored.

There was a swimming pool in the courtyard of my motel. Its water was chlorinated, but I had enough packets that I could turn it to salt if I wished.

Four dozen Jenny Hanivers, all bearing my name, rotted in the trunk of my car. They called to me through gaping dead mouths. They wanted to take me home.

My limbs tingled and tingled and tingled. So much I could barely make it out of my room, down the steps, into the courtyard and the lip of the pool. I fell to the tiles and pushed over the edge. A little further now. Only a little further.

I wanted to wake. The water would wake me. The water would claim me. The mermaid's dream would end.

The Jenny Hanivers rotted. The moon shone down. The pool was calm and still.

Somewhere, beneath the cold crush of tides, my heart is wrapped in seaweed, chained to the ocean floor.

THE ROAR OF THE GREASEPAINT

R. MICHAEL BURNS

Zilch sat alone in the cracker-box makeup trailer and stared at his face in the mirror, moon-pale and framed by naked bulbs that shaded too much toward yellow. The rest of the floppy-shoe brigade had already changed and headed off to hit the closest dive in whatever-the-hell town they'd crash-landed in this week, determined to get laid if they could or wildly trashed if they couldn't. But old Zilch just couldn't muster the enthusiasm for that stale chase anymore—couldn't muster much enthusiasm for anything these days.

He stared at the absurd thing gazing back at him from three feet beyond the glass. Bald but for the yellow tufts of hair jutting out over each ear, eyes framed by big points-down crescent moons, also yellow, that made him look cynical and vaguely angry. Fat orange nose like the capillary-blasted schnoz of a lifelong boozer. And that crazy greasepaint grin, yellow too, from cheek to cheek, as if he had a banana clenched in his teeth.

What a clown.

He offered his mirror-self a grin. It reciprocated with a rictus leer that made him quit. Too many deep lines there, dragging down the lips, entrenching those lifeless peepers, hollowing the cheeks. White paint couldn't hide all those years on the road.

Not anymore.

He picked up the hand towel, the jar of cold cream, dabbed at the stuff and raised the cloth to his brow.

A shiver shot through the very core of him, sudden and clutching as a jolt of electricity. The towel fell in a lump on the table.

He closed his eyes against his ghastly glass-trapped image.

Midway memories poured into his mind to fill the dark, gusted through from twenty years ago or blew in as fresh as the sawdust on his oversized shoes. All the rip-off games in their clapboard booths – *hey mistuh, just hook the ring on that bottle and win your kid a prize, huh?* – and the groan of the Erector Set rides – Tilt-a-Whirl, and carousel, and electric-spitting bumper cars sang their own songs. The wafted odors of popcorn and cotton candy, so thick they saturated the lungs and made your stomach churn after hours with no escape. All the dazzle of the naked glass bulbs strung overhead like beads of dew on a spider web; the insect-hum of neon, the crunch of dirt and weeds trampled underfoot. Shills shouting up audiences for The Astounding Arioldis and Miraculous Marcus and Morganna the Uncanny. The flap of tent-canvas in the evening breeze, the stink of animal manure. And the people, so damn many people – dads grumbling over how much all this cost, corndog here, spook house there; put-upon girlfriends fending off clumsy drunken passes from their beer-goggled guys; kids shoving each other around to get just that much closer to the front of the line, whatever line, it didn't even matter.

R. MICHAEL BURNS

Had there ever been even a hint of magic, even a glim-
mer of merriment in any of it? Zilch rubbed his temples
and tried to conjure the least trace of joy from the debris
of his life as a carny. People coming, going, vanishing.
A new fire eater, a new group of surly teamster types to
rivet the rides back together. Pimply kids that shuffled
in and out of the game booths, the concessions stands.
Lots of forgotten towns, vacant fields, strip-mall parking
lots. A few hundred patrons a day, multiplied by a thousand days, and all of them exactly the same no matter the
place, no matter the year.

And yet he *had* felt some foolish attachment to the
carnival scene once, hadn't he? Not to the life, the vaga-
bond existence, his home an RV most people would've
been ashamed to park in a hidden wilderness, his every
meal eaten in the roadside places even the long-haul
truckers avoided. But to the *scene*, that dreamlike world
of candy-striped tents under rainbow-glow lights, Ferris
wheel forever taking passengers nowhere, carousel whirling in its endless steeplechase...hell, even those junk food
fragrances that now nearly made him gag. And most, the
strange absurd power of the performance, of jumping
into the fray and clowning, of pratfalls and pies in the
face, the bright sound of laughter, the big dopey grins.

Sure. Maybe. Maybe some other him, some younger,
vacuous him had really relished all that, basked in the
neon, drunk in the noise, puffed himself up on the frantic
frenetic energy of it. But he'd left that kid, the one who
hadn't needed to fake his smile, somewhere far behind,
in Podunk, Idaho, or Hicksburg, Illinois, or Nowheres-
ville, Kansas. Sometime while he'd schlepped from town
to town, he'd dumped that goggling idiot the way a man
abandons an unwanted cur. All the same, he stuck with
the gig and plodded his way from shtick to shtick, painting on a smile he couldn't begin to feel, almost etching it

into his flesh just to keep it in place. What the hell else could he do at his age? Take up accountancy? Sell used cars? What – and give up show business?

He smirked. It was as much of a laugh as he could manage these days.

God, that thing in the mirror looked dreadful. A corpse badly made-up by a hack undertaker.

He picked up the cold-creamed rag again, touched it to his cheek – and again, dropped it.

No. He didn't want to see whatever lurked under that paint tonight, didn't want to see the cadaver stripped of its last hint of garish pseudo-life. Just the thought of his waxen complexion without that false smile, without that splash of artificial color, made him a bit queasy. More than that – scared the hell out of him.

Zilch and his glass doppelganger grimaced at one another. Was that the look he gave the crowds these days? No wonder the littlest kids frowned and turned away.

He shook his head at that grim thing in the frame of sallow lights – the bogeyman from some kid's nightmare, a thing that belonged in the closet, under the bed, in the shadows. And beneath the makeup? His hands clenched tight on the makeup counter.

Things had gotten nasty lately – the gags, the jokes. No more lighthearted slapstick, dropping the fake barbell on his oversized toes, slipping on the handy banana peel. These days he got his laughs with abuse, mocking the gawkers, their postures and mannerisms, shooting water in their eyes from the moldy old fake flower on his lapel. Cheap tricks, all derision and cruelty scarcely masked beneath that big yellow grin.

Tonight, the whole shtick had twisted right out of his grasp. He'd been at the same tired game, aping a drunken kid in a tattered muscle-shirt, copying with garish exaggeration the alcohol-clumsy way the kid ambled with one arm slung around his girlfriend's shoulders, his hand idly groping at the pimply blonde's chest. Zilch had seen the first flash of irritation in the kid's half-lidded eyes, but it hadn't bothered him one bit, because he was getting the laughs. Never mind that half the giggles sounded stiff as cardboard and badly uncomfortable, and that the rest had a mean-spirited edge to them. He got paid to give the rubes on the midway a good chuckle – hell, he *lived* to give 'em a few hoots. The quality and kind of the laughter didn't matter a damn bit, not these days. So he returned the kid's fuck-you glare with a couple hundred percent interest. The kid dropped his arm from the blonde's shoulders and took an unstable step forward, glowering now. Zilch scrunched his eyes, lowered his head, set his jaw and pouted his lips, took an answering step toward the kid and raised his fists, wagging them in the air like a boxer in an old cartoon.

"You think you're funny, man?" the kid drawled.

Zilch frowned, scratched his bald dome thoughtfully, then stuck out his tongue and let loose with a long wet raspberry.

The crowd dribbling past gave a murmur of uncertain laughter – and the blonde giggled. That pretty much finished it with Mr. Muscle-shirt.

"The fuck you laughin' at, Justine?" he asked the girl.

"You're bein' a total jerk, Jason," the girl answered. "No wonder this guy's makin' fun of you."

"Fuck you, Justine. And fuck you too, you asshole."

The kid turned then, taking a big roundhouse swing as he did, the kind of punch only a bad actor or a drunken idiot would throw. Zilch ducked it with comic ease and came back up in his bouncing, pseudo-pugilistic stance, even as the crowd, gathering now, chortled again. Dear Justine laughed right along with them. The kid snarled and swung again. Zilch leaned, watched the fist swish past, then bobbed back and blew the kid a kiss.

The crowd, pumped up on Mr. Muscle-shirt's humiliation, cackled now, as did the girlfriend. Zilch turned
and gave a deep, sweeping bow to the neon-lit faces, all
scythe-blade grins and glass-hard leers.

The kid lurched at him again, predictable as the sunset. Zilch stepped aside and let the kid fall flat on his face.
Mr. Muscle-shirt hit the dirty midway with a soft, wet
crunch, and lay there limp as a wet rag.

For just an instant, Zilch froze, staring at the prone
kid, icewater pumping through his veins. It had all finally
gone too damn far. The kid was hurt, maybe even unconscious. Nothing funny in this, in any of it. The clown
looked up, looked into the gawking crowd for help –
surely someone would step forward, check the kid out,
maybe give a shout for the first aid guys.

But the crowd didn't glare accusation at him. They
didn't look shocked or startled or worried. No one
stooped to the kid's side saying *hey man you okay?* Instead
they all beamed at Zilch, their smiles as huge and gaudy
as his greasepaint grin, then applauded raucously. The
girl guffawed and wiped tears of laughter off her pimply
cheeks, smeared her makeup so she looked bruised. Every sight, every sound and smell stood out double, triple
bright, stretched out and warped like comics copied on
Silly-Putty, hideous, crazy.

Zilch ogled them, thunderstruck – then clenched his
hands and held them up over his head, waved them the
way a champion prizefighter might after a solid K.O. The
crowd howled. The clown rolled his arm and took a deep
bow, and another, and another. He was still bowing as
Mr. Muscle-shirt picked himself up one limb at a time,
muttering that he'd broken his nose, he'd broken his fug-
gin' nose, goddabbit.

With a flurry of catcalls and wolf-whistles, the audience broke up and drifted off toward the funnel cake booth, the Round-Up, the Pitch-n-Win. Zilch made a show of following a couple of gabby pubescent girls, walking on tip-toes with his big white gloves outstretched in the manner of a melodrama villain, ready to tap them on the shoulders, both-at-once, and watch them jump, hear them squeal.

Through it all, he'd remained hidden behind the makeup, the foolish costume, the fake hair. Never turned back into a real person who'd get mad or drop the jokes and walk away. Never let the gag drop, even when the kid's nose went crunch – not for anything more than that barest split second of naked fear, hardly long enough to blink an eye.

Tomorrow, mean jokes and mockery, same as today. More little kids shrinking back when he waved at them. More blood in the dirt? Sure, why the hell not? All fun and laughs until someone gets hurt, his mother used to say. And after someone got hurt? The ugly reality of laughter – comedy is watching pain happen to someone else.

But the hell with that – the hell with *all* of it. The day was dead and laid to rest. Time to scrape off the fake grin and flop into bed until tomorrow's cast call when he'd revive the whole farce yet again, an absurd Frankenstein raising an even more ludicrous monster.

Zilch picked up the cold-cream slicked rag once more, but even as he lifted it to one white cheek, his fingers clenched down on it as if in a spasm of sudden, premature rigor mortis. Fear gushed through his chest, deep and drowning, intense as childhood's worst nightmare.

Don't, man, just...don't, some frantic voice pleaded, deep in his skull. *Don't dig up the wasted man buried under the clown-white, the banana-yellow. Leave the corpse in its grave, for fuck's sake.*

But that? That was crazy, wasn't it? The jittery paranoia of a nutjob, the terror of a madman? He'd gone through the same ritual on a thousand other nights. Hell, he'd done it just last night.

Funny, though, he couldn't really remember last night. Couldn't really remember the makeup trailer, the light bulb-encircled mirror, the greasy rag. Couldn't remember anything beyond the midway. And the night before? Or before that? Shadows, vague, dark, shapeless.

He sat with the cloth vice-gripped in his fist, frozen solid a mere inch from his flesh, and stared at the thing staring at him from the icy depths of the silvered glass.

The girl's pitiless cackles. The kid's nose going crunch. The crowd, all applause and cheers, gorging itself on humiliation. It all bounced around inside Zilch's skull like shrapnel.

Enough. No more.

No more gags, no more cruel humor, no more dehumanizing play. Not the next day, not next week, not ever. Time to get out – peddle cheap insurance, sell shoes, whatever the hell it took. Just walk away from the tents and the rides and the wild animal odors, all of it. Hang that face up for good and let old Zilch the Clown fade into the shadows like the ghost he'd so long ago become. He could finally take back the name his parents had given him, the one his friends had called him by, back when he'd had friends. It was long past time for all of that, really, but surely it wasn't too late, not yet....

But – why couldn't he remember last night? Why couldn't he remember taking this hateful makeup off?

Mechanical as an automaton, his hand moved the last inch, rubbed cloth to flesh, hard, like a cabinet maker removing varnish with sandpaper, scraping. In daubs and streaks, the vivid white began to vanish, revealing a ghastlier colorlessness beneath, skin that hadn't seen the sun in far too long, the pallor of a dead man badly embalmed. He rubbed away the edges of his grin, scrubbed his dimples off with two hard swipes, obliterated his eyebrows. With a sick yet distant dread, he stared as the clown-thing in the mirror erased its mouth, lips and all, leaving behind a featureless blank, unbroken from chin to nose. Mindless fingers plucked off the big yellow sponge ball, exposed the nothing-at-all beneath. And still he watched, mesmerized, as gloved clown hands took him apart piece by piece, their movement automatic, unthinking. They tore free the tufts of hair, peeled bone-white ears from a smooth white skull. Nearly done, sure, but not quite. Not wiped clean yet. He gazed in dull wonder as that claw with its greasepaint-bright rag scrubbed away one eye, watched somehow as the other eye went, too, as old Zilch did the best damned vanishing act ever, replaced by this non-creature he'd secretly suspected for some long while now. He'd flensed away the very last of the clown – the only identity left to him smeared and growing tacky in the crumpled towel. Whoever had lived behind the paint had faded into oblivion months ago, or years. Dead in some weed-wild lot somewhere, rotting along with the yellow newspapers and the cigarette butts. Dead and haunting that baggy clown suit, that false grin, all those soulless midways.

Eyeless, he sat and stared into the garishly-lit glass emptiness for a very long time.

THE CARNIVAL'S CHILDREN

J.T. EVANS

I crept through the sagging gates of the rusted, portable fence and kept an eye out for movement. I couldn't see very far this night because of the new moon, and the comforting glow of Pittsburgh's city lights fell dark a week ago. *It's amazing how fast the world fell to shit after the C.L.O.W.N.S. appeared.*

I hated roaming the city at night, but there was no choice this time. Normally, my team and I hunted C.L.O.W.N.S. during the day when they're blinded by the brilliance of the sun. At night, we sheltered in a fortified warehouse surrounded by barbed wire. Some of our engineers worked on other defenses, but they're not done with the bunkers and machine gun mounts yet.

This time, we were out wandering the inky darkness looking for a child. Margot spotted the little girl wandering around the abandoned carnival just before sunset. She said the girl wore a blue dress with yellow flowers on it. Aria, Larry, Mike, Fred and I pulled the assignment to track down the little one and bring her safely back to the warehouse.

I moved ten feet past the gate, did another scan, spotting nothing. I waved a hand over my shoulder. The rustling of the chain link fence told me the rest of my team had followed me into the dead carnival. I waited until the crunch of gravel beneath combat boots neared my back. In a low whisper, I said, "We gotta search this whole place, but I don't want to split up."

Aria said, "Yeah. There's no telling how many CLOWNS are roaming inside here."

Christ, I loved the way she said the word. I could hear the acronym flow from her tongue like honey dripping from a biscuit. C-L-O-W-N-S.

A scientist somewhere identified the process as a strange pathogen in makeup and face paints shipped over from China. He called it, "Cognitive Loss from Overnight Withering of Neurological Synapses." God does have a sense of humor. Now if He had just worked the platypus into the equation somewhere, it would fall into the down-right-hilarious category.

The same scientist told educated the public about people with C.L.O.W.N.S.. He said the afflicted were reduced to their most basic instincts of survival. I remember something about a "lizard brain" or something like that. He was boring. I didn't pay that much attention to the reports.

Circus and rodeo clowns weren't the only people afflicted by the tainted makeup. It struck at Halloween, so children, parents, partygoers, and anyone else celebrating the holiday became horrible creatures trying to eat anything moving. I've even heard rumors that women's makeup carried the infectious crap. It makes me wonder how many movie stars and television personalities that pack the stuff on before going on camera are now roaming the nights trying to feast upon those of us who are still normal.

I snapped out of my thoughts and replied, "We're in an abandoned, traveling carnival, so assume there will be plenty. Everyone keep your weapons ready." We all carried sharp, hand-to-hand weapons. In the first week after the Night of Madness, good Hunters learned that using firearms was practically worthless against an afflicted person. The loud report of a gun did nothing more than attract attention to the shooter's location. It's bloody work to kill a clown up close and personal. At least the pathogen in the makeup isn't contagious.

After looking at the skeletal fingers of rides and the gigantic Ferris wheel, I made a quick plan of action. "We'll start here at the gate and work our way in a tightening spiral to the middle of the carnival. It looks like-"

"Shit!" Mike screamed out as a clown flew out of the night toward us. The darkness made it hard to see details, but the flopping red wig and smeared white pancake makeup marked the creature as a former clown. Even as I hefted the weight of my axe, I wondered how much joy it had inspired in children and how much dread in the adults. The red paint surrounding the clown's mouth further accentuated the creep factor as it spread its jaw as wide as it could go.

Mike brought up a machete and swung at the clown's neck with all his might, but an upraised arm caught the blow. As the forearm and hand spiraled off into the night to land with a wet thud, the clown slammed into Mike and drove him to the ground. He twisted left and right to keep his face from being eaten off by the madman.

Aria raced forward with a Chinese broadsword in her hands, but couldn't get a clear swing with the heavy blade. I pounded on the clown's back with the butt of my axe in hopes of distracting it, and Larry just stood there dumbfounded. He always was the last to move his massive bulk.

Mike screamed out, "Do something!" as he continued to dodge gnashing teeth.

The sound of several hissing C.L.O.W.N.S. sounded in the darkness. Mike had attracted their attention.

"Damn it," I called out. "Form a circle. We've got incoming!"

Mike's voice raised an octave. "What about me?"

As calm as the day is long, Fred said, "I thought you had it in hand. Let me help." He stepped forward and drew one knife in a smooth motion. He watched the rise and fall of the clown's head for a few seconds while the rest of us formed a protective perimeter around Mike. Finally, Fred lunged forward, stuck the knife's blade across the clown's throat and pulled hard.

The former clown thrashed and sprayed blood that looked black in the night. Before the clown's body stopped twitching, Mike kicked free, stood up, and spit the clown's blood from his mouth. "You could have at least turned it to the side before you slit its throat."

Fred flashed an evil grin at Mike. "Next time I'll just let it eat you."

Mike moved to face the new wave of C.L.O.W.N.S.. "Ha. Ha. Very funny."

Three figures lurched out of the darkness. Two of them were children that made up a Raggedy Anne and Andy set, and the third was another carnival clown.

Double damn it. I remember those kids. Time to get a little revenge.

I snarled, "Aria and Larry on the Big Guy. Mike and Fred, you take Little Andy. That bitch, Raggedy Anne, is all mine."

Starlight glinted off of steel as the C.L.O.W.N.S.

hissed their desire to feast on our flesh. I kept the rest of the combat in my peripheral vision as I attracted Anne's attention toward me. She peeled away from her brother and charged with bared teeth. Her pearly whites weren't so white anymore. Gore covered them, and bits of skin, presumably human, stuck out between her teeth.

Man, she needs to floss.

I circled away from her charge and brought the handle of my axe up to catch her in the chin. From past experience, I knew C.L.O.W.N.S. could feel a small amount of pain, but it rarely slowed them down. In this case, all I did was snap back Anne's head and flip her to the ground.

She never paused, and used the momentum I had given her to roll on the ground and spring back upright. I readied for another charge with my axe in a ready-to-swing position. Anne ran at me again. I shifted the grip on my axe and slammed the butt of the handle into her forehead. This stunned her long enough for me to hit her twice more. Normally, I'd dispatch someone with C.L.O.W.N.S. in the most expedient method at hand, but I had some payback to give to this little bitch. This was my chance.

Anne recovered from my blows and reached for my left leg.

I danced back. "Not again, you little whore!"

She continued to reach down at my knee as if some distant memory compelled her to bite me in the same place again. I took advantage of the situation and slammed the blunt side of my axe's head into the top of her skull. A satisfying wet crunching sound spat forth from between her ears. Anne fell to the ground and twitched from the blow. That wasn't good enough for me. I had to finish her, and not with the usual method of decapitation.

I knelt on her chest and slammed the top of my axe

into her face over and over. Rasping breaths exploded from my lungs, and I put everything I had into the death of this vile little creature lying on the ground under my knee.

Before I knew it, Mike's strong hands pulled me from the pulped corpse. He stepped back from my glare with his hands up in the air. "Whoa. Whoa. Easy, man. What's that all aboot, eh?" His "Hockey Night in Canada" accent snapped me back to reality.

I pointed down at the bloody mess of Anne's face. "You won't recognize her now, but she's that little bitch that attacked me on Halloween night when all this shit started."

Aria looked down at the mess I had made of the little girl's face. "She attacked you? Why didn't you kill her like any one else with C.L.O.W.N.S.?"

I shrugged. "It was the start of the Night of Madness. We didn't know what was going on. No one did. Mike and Fred were there. It was Halloween and three of us were playing poker at my place. Like always, I answered the door when the bell rang. A family stood there. Dad was the Grim Reaper. Mom was a *hot* Dorothy from Oz, and the kids were, well, these two little shits." I pointed down at Anne and the decapitated Andy.

"That one," I pointed at Andy, "ate his own mother's face off before running into the night. Dad jumped on me and tried to choke me out while that little bitch," I pointed at Anne, "tried to chew my kneecap off."

I shook my head to clear out the memories of two months ago. "If it wasn't for Mike and Fred being at my place when all this went down, I'd have been clown food that night. That's why I hate them so damn much. They scare me to my very core, and I have to channel that fear into hatred just to stay alive."

Aria gently put her hand on my arm. Lightning shot up and down my spine, and the feeling intensified as she smiled at me. "I get it, Ray. I really do. I hunt for the same reasons. You got your revenge on Anne tonight. I can only hope I find the clown that killed my mother and father and put an end to it. I just don't know which one it was. I figure if I kill all of them, then I'll know that the fucker that ate my parents is dead and gone."

I put my hand on top of Aria's. "We'll do our best to stand by your side."

Larry pulled his Pittsburgh Pirates hat from his head and wiped the sweat from his brow. "Get a room! We're here to save a little girl, not make-out like teenagers."

Aria pulled her hand from arm and shot Larry a glare. "We weren't… oh… you…." She closed her mouth as words escaped her.

I pinched the bridge of my nose with a finger and thumb and squeezed my eyes tight. "Larry's right. We gotta find this little girl and get outta here before more C.L.O.W.N.S.. find us. I was going to say we should spiral inward from the outer fence to the innermost areas. That should let us cover all of the ground without missing anything."

We worked our way around the steel, plastic and rubber constructs of the dead carnival looking for the child. We searched under bunting, peered under flaps, and thoroughly searched. For fear of attracting more people with C.L.O.W.N.S., we didn't call out or yell for the little girl. For all we knew, she was scared and in deep hiding. Hell, she could even be somewhere entirely different now.

Fred echoed my thoughts with a whisper, "I don't think she's around here."

Aria replied, "We have to keep looking. I wouldn't leave any of you behind. I won't leave a frightened little girl behind either."

I said, "Aria's got it right. We keep looking. Just be alert."

As we made our way closer to the center of the carnival, we came across a group of mostly-deflated bouncy houses. One house, a purple castle, bounced and rolled like two cats in a wet sack. I hefted my axe and prepared to lop off some clown heads as I approached the giant balloon-like structure. I stuck out one hand and peeled back the first layer of fabric. Nothing. Using the head of my axe to catch more folds of cloth, I pulled back to make the opening larger. The faint sound of moaning and hissing filtered out from between the collapsed layers of fabric. I didn't know what to expect, so I glanced back at my team. They stood ready to strike at anything springing forth from the tangled mess.

I worked my way through the folds and layers until I finally came across a sight that I hope never repeats itself in my life as a Hunter.

Two people with C.L.O.W.N.S. fucked what was left of their brains out amidst the happy purple castle's remains.

I stood frozen with puzzlement and disgust.

The infected man's pasty-white ass pumped up and down. With each thrust, balls slapped wetly sound against the cottage-cheese rear end of the woman beneath him. He grunted with each advance of his cock, and the woman moaned in pleasure at the pounding she received. I hadn't uncovered her head yet, and they hadn't seemed to notice me. I reached over their sweaty bodies with my trusty axe and uncovered the rest of the sex scene unfolding before my eyes.

I heard Mike ask, "What are you doing, eh?"

I didn't answer him. My astonishment took over

as the next bit of repulsion appeared. The woman only moaned because her mouth was full of another man's flaccid member. My non-virginal mind immediately went someplace I didn't want it to. *Well, at least she won't gag on that.*

I shook my head to clear the amazement. There weren't *two* infected people down there romping on each other. The final fold of fabric had concealed yet *another* dude getting his tiny dick sucked on by the woman. It was like watching a Chinese finger trap in action. But with clowns... and fucking... and sucking.

The ball-slapping sound set a rhythm I could almost dance to, and the woman gobbled the man-beef for all she was worth. I stared for a moment longer before coming to my senses. I didn't know if these creatures of my nightmares could cum or not, but I wasn't about to wait around to find out.

I sighed.

I hated to cock block anyone, even someone with C.L.O.W.N.S., but as soon as the threesome came to an end, they'd get up hungry and try to eat my face. I couldn't have that.

I stepped to one side and trapped a roll of the castle's wall under my foot. With my free hand, I waved the group over and motioned down at the orgy going on below me.

I watched their faces and reactions shift from concern to curiosity to amazement and finally to disgust. Larry turned to one side, gagged a few times and hurled all over the pavement.

Aria danced sideways as some of the puke landed on her boots. "Damn it, Larry. Now I have to.... Oh, never mind. It's just puke covering clown blood."

I whispered, "We can't leave them here. Gotta take them out before they get bored with this and eat someone."

Everyone, except Larry, nodded in agreement. He was still caught up in the middle of more retching, and the team slid a little further away from him.

I adjusted the grip on my axe and shuffled another two feet to my right to clear the way for another person. I motioned for Mike to step up with his machete. Fred stood back a bit with his twin Bowie knives. I pointed at myself and the woman. Then I pointed at Mike and the first guy I exposed. Then I made little "run away" motions with two of my fingers, and pointed at Fred and the second guy.

Once everyone was on the same page of the plan, I whispered, "On three," and held up a finger. Then two. I turned my focus to the woman's neck and shifted the grip on my axe. As I held up the third finger, Mike sprung into action.

The Canadian stepped forward and swung the machete like he meant for the clown's head to fly to the fences. The breeze from his blade swept past my bare arms just before impacting the man's neck exactly halfway between the shoulders and the base of the skull. A fountain of blood shot into the air as the head rolled clear of the stump. Mike used the blade's momentum to carry his body wide of the slumping corpse, and I filled the space he just vacated.

Placing my own inertia behind my swing, I brought my axe down on the woman's throat before she reacted to her lover's death. The blade bit deep into flesh, but I didn't have the right angle for the attack. The blade stuck into her spine and caused her to convulse and spray arterial blood in a shuddering fan that covered my legs and torso in the vile stuff. Mike stepped clear of the whole mess, and I followed suit. I left my beloved axe behind.

Feeling somewhat naked without my primary weapon, I drew a knife similar to the pair Fred carried.

The final clown suddenly realized his knob was no longer being polished and rolled out from under the slip of fabric that covered his face. A grotesque visage revealed itself. The left half of its face had been melted away by acid or flame, and its lower jaw hung loose. Only the right side was still attached, and even then only a thin cord of sinew held it in place. The clown vocalized a guttural sound halfway between the gurgle of a drowning child and the rumbling chuff of a pissed off grizzly bear. The smell of rotting flesh and whisky-hangover breath washed over me. Cloudy eyes stared about with smoldering anger. He stood amongst the dying bodies of his lovers, and glared at each of us in turn.

Fred didn't dare step in on the uncertain footing of the blood and gore covering the fabric of the collapsed castle. Instead, he waited for the clown to approach.

The nightmare took the bait and lunged.

Fred timed his attack perfectly. He swiped his twin blades in a scissoring motion across the thing's neck. Its head fell away as the body crashed into my teammate. Fred took the weight as if he had been expecting it and shifted it away from him using a basic Judo maneuver.

Mike raised his machete in the air to signal victory. "I hope I never have to see anything like that again.

Larry came up for air from his puking session. "What the fuck was that? Why were they…?"

Aria shrugged. "My pops always told me stupid creatures in life see other things as either edible or fuckable. If they can't do one or the other to it, then piss on it. I think he was mainly talking about our dog, but I'm not sure."

Fred frowned. "I think there's more to it than that. Maybe something along the lines of –"

The Carnival's Children

The shrill sound of an animal shrieking in pain pierced the night and brought our conversation to a halt.

I leaped into the mess of the purple castle and fetched my axe as the team ran toward the sounds of a tortured animal. I ran behind them and eventually caught up using my longer stride. As we turned the corner around a cotton candy booth, the yowls of pain cut off and left us standing there in an eerie silence.

A small form, barely visible in the depths of the night, sat on the ground about ten feet away with something in its lap. A small puddle of darkness spread out on the ground. I squinted in an effort to make out details, but none would come to me. I opened my mouth to ask a question when the world lit up.

I managed to get out, "What the fuck?" as strands of overhead light bulbs illuminated the world around us.

Rides turned on. Gears ground and caught on one another to force motion into the carriages, coasters and flipping cages. Wheels squealed in protest and almost drowned out the hollow, tinny music echoing forth from hidden speakers. Somewhere nearby, the canned laugh of a demented clown came the fun house and rang across the carnival. The area came to life… almost. The cheerful chatter, bellowing children, gleeful laughter, and pitter-patter of feet on the asphalt left an empty hole in the otherwise normal setting. A chill thundered up my back as I realized someone must have figured out how to restore power to at least part of Pittsburgh. I looked out over the city's skyline and saw that nearby streetlights and buildings had lit up. In the distance, however, things remained dark.

This turn of events would make most people feel more comfortable out at night. The lights would lead to more encounters with the C.L.O.W.N.S., and we Hunters would be as busy as ever.

The little girl interrupted my thoughts about the future.

She craned her neck up at an unnatural angle to look at us. "Kitty tastes *good*." With the last word, her voice went from the prepubescent high octaves of a child to the depths of tone usually associated with sailors with a two-pack-a-day habit for the last twenty years. I looked closer. The pale complexion sitting underneath the red blotch of faded paint told me one thing for sure.

She had C.L.O.W.N.S..

Damn it. I've already had to kill one child tonight. Why another?

Another detail slammed home. Her dress. Even though it was covered in the fresh blood of the cat she just killed, the blue pattern and yellow flowers shone through. We were sent here to rescue this poor soul, and now we have to banish from this world.

Larry must have come to the same realization I did because he cracked his neck like he usually before a fight and drew his falchion from its scabbard.

Before any of could move, the girl in the flowery dress launched herself at Aria. Larry moved his bulk into the child's path and thrust the point of his blade into her throat. Blood fountained from the wound, staining the front of her blue dress.

The rest of us finally snapped into action and we surrounded the snarling, gurgling girl. She leaped at each of us in turn, but we always corralled her back to the center of our circle. She never relented, tired, or gave up. After a minute of this, sweat covered all of us despite the chill of the night. Cuts, deep and shallow, covered the child's body, but she kept coming.

None of us were able to land a killing blow. I don't

think any of us *wanted* to kill this seemingly innocent creature. However, we all knew that we *had* to put it... her down. I felt like that young boy from Old Yeller when his dog contracted rabies. Even though I didn't know this little girl, I saw the promise of growth, intelligence and a future in her. Cheap Chinese face paint took all of this away from her.

Anger seethed within me. I defended myself from another leap, and my rage boiled over. I couldn't stand it any further. It had to end this poor thing's suffering.

As the girl retreated from me yet again, I bellowed out a harsh cry and struck down with all my might. This time, instead of lodging my axe into the spine, the blade swung clean through and removed the girl's head from her shoulders. More blood filled the air, and meaty, wet thump that I'd grown all too familiar with sounded as the decapitated head hit the ground.

I dropped my axe and sat on the ground. Unbidden tears came. I let them. It might be a sign of weakness for a guy to cry in front of his Hunter team, but fuck it. I needed this cry. I've seen too much violence for my days, and it's only been two months since C.L.O.W.N.S. infected millions, maybe billions, of people.

My team stood by me as I let loose. Tears and snot flowed down my face until I finally got it out of my system. Once I finished cleansing my soul with my own tears, I wiped my face on my grime-covered t-shirt. I'm sure it didn't help my appearance much, but I didn't care.

I recovered my axe and stood up. "Let's go home. I'm tired of hunting tonight. We'll pick up our patrol where we left off come morning."

No one said a thing as we walked away from the clumsy clanking and horrid screeching of the carnival's active machines.

I threw one last, furtive glance over my shoulder at the carnival's carcass. The lights and sounds of the hulking behemoth had attracted more people with C.L.O.W.N.S.. Their familiar, lurching movements peeked out the shadows of the ramshackle buildings and dilapidated rides as we walked away. I briefly thought about turning my team around to take more of them out, but I'd had enough for one night.

The dimming lights and hollow sounds of the carnival faded away as we walked home to the warehouse.

Printed in Great Britain
by Amazon